THE CCC

Who really runs America?

Chuck Kimball

The CCC

Chuck Kimball

Library of Congress Control Number: 2020925884

HARDBACK: 978-1-953791-97-9
PAPERBACK: 978-1-953791-96-2
EBOOK: 978-1-953791-98-6

Ordering Information:

For orders and inquiries, please contact:
1-888-404-1388
www.goldtouchpress.com
book.orders@goldtouchpress.com

Printed in the United States of America

CHAPTER 1
Afghanistan, July 2020

ABOUT FIFTY MILES EAST OF KOH-E HINDU, DEEP INTO the mountains, a special operations group of seven men lay hidden. They had been there, behind the boulders, for close to a week watching a group of Taliban fighters training. As soon as the military organization would move, the special ops group would follow, waiting until the opportunity arose to take them out.

Sergeant Rich Ferguson was lying on his back with his head resting against his pack. Without warning, he felt someone shake his shoulder and say, "Wake up, you have a call from HQ." Rich took a deep breath, opened and closed his eyes a few times, wiped his goggles off, and took the phone from his second in command. On the phone, he introduced himself and gave his operations code number. Rich listened to the caller, never interrupting, then after a few minutes, spoke, "Yes sir. Thirty klicks south in the valley at fourteen hundred." He held the handset for a minute, then turned to Rod, his second-in-command, "I have to leave in a few minutes. I guess you heard where I am going."

"I did."

"I will be met by a Sikorsky UH-60 Black Hawk. The lieutenant has further orders from HQ for me. I know nothing else. You are in command old friend, and while I am gone, don't do anything that I wouldn't do." Rich then leaned over and gave his old buddy a brotherly hug and a slap on the back. Without another word, he picked up his gear, walked by each of his men, shook their hand, and wished them luck, promising he would see them soon. Little did he know that he would never see them again on the battlefield.

It was a long, hot, dry, and dusty four-hour walk until he reached the valley on the other side of the ridge. His handkerchief was covered with sweat and brown stains from wiping his face during the long trek from the rocky mountains to the open valley below. As he arrived at the indicated meeting place, he heard the Black Hawk's rotor blades flying in low down the valley. Five minutes later, the threatening-looking blackbird sat down in front of him with its guns and missiles pointing outward. The side door opened. A man dressed in fatigues stepped out and reached behind him for a heavy pack he placed on his back. He grabbed an automatic weapon that he kept in his hand.

Rich squinted his eyes into the sun, wondering why the Lt. was dressed in fatigues and equipped for combat. He did not salute as he walked up to his old friend, this being the custom in war. Rich stuck out his hand for a firm handshake.

The Lt. announced," I have not got much time. I am taking over your op. Here are your new orders. You are to read them on the bird on your way to Kabul."

Rich could not refrain from giving away his astonishment. He took the brown sealed envelope stamped Top Secret. "What the hell is going on? Why am I heading back to Kabul?"

"I have no idea. Get going, sergeant. I have to head up the hill and be with my group by dark. Good luck." The Lt. reached out his hand for a quick handshake and headed up the dusty brown ridge.

Still confused, Rich walked with his head down and entered the Bell Arapaho. Once aboard and locked into his seat, the blackbird lifted off and headed toward Kabul. At the start of the almost three-hour flight, Rich opened the sealed large envelope. He looked at the letterhead on the first page. It included acronyms that did not jog his memory. A bit anxious, Rich blew air through his teeth and started reading. The orders were from a familiar officer, Colonel Coleman, a man he admired, a fatherly figure who had given him his first sergeant stripes. Somewhat relieved, he began to read the contents: Your twenty-year retirement request was approved seventeen months early. Benefits will be discussed later. After you have gone through the usual medical procedures at Bergen Air Force Base in Germany, you will fly to your old unit in South Carolina. All paperwork was processed and ready for you. You will then fly commercial within forty-eight hours to Washington DC. Address of your hotel below. Your meeting place and time are included. See you soon. Rich finished reading the rest of the orders, then leaned back, closed his eyes, and relaxed to the blades' rhythm.

Rich woke up just before touching down at the airbase in Kabul. Once given the OK, he exited the helicopter. As he entered the Quonset building, another acquaintance, Captain Gerry Robinson, walked toward Rich. "Well, Sarge, what's so important in that secret package that I had to send a chopper for a special delivery?"

"Hold on a minute, Cap, until we can hear better." In the office, the two men talked for a minute or so. "Rich, don't sit down. You have forty-five minutes to get the rest of your stuff and be on the bird to Germany. I don't know what's going on, but I wish you good luck, and I am glad to hear you are getting out of this hell hole.

TWO WEEKS LATER

CHAPTER 2
Washington DC

THE UNITED AIRLINES FLIGHT ATTENDANT HAD WALKED by seat 1A numerous times. Sitting there was a well-built gentleman about six feet, maybe six-one, with prominent tanned muscles. With his head uncomfortably resting on a pillow placed against the small window, he seemed to be sleeping. His shortcut light brown hair looked as if he had just combed it. The flight attendant stopped in the aisle and leaned forward to look out the man's window. She could see a cold misty fog was hovering above the Nation's capital. All of a sudden, the flight captain made an announcement, "Prepare for landing." Minutes later, one could hear a loud grinding sound followed by a bang as the landing gear locked in place. Soon afterward, the big bird bounced once, then again, as the wheels made contact with the runway at Reagan International airport in Washington, DC.

The man sitting alone in the first row moved over to the aisle seat. When the seatbelt sign went off, he stretched his six-foot-plus frame before opening the overhead storage bin. Reaching in, he brought out his black leather jacket and a soft brown leather pack. Rich fitted the strap of the luggage over his left shoulder and draped his jacket over his left arm. As soon as the flight attendant gave the go-ahead, he stepped forward. As she looked into his bright blue eyes, she became speechless—she pointed, then whispered, "Have a good evening."

He was now on his way to meet Colonel Coleman. On the drive, the closer he got to his destination, the fewer the cars on the road. There were few late-night wanderers on the sidewalk, some vagrants pushing shopping carts loaded with their belongings, and what looked like ladies of the night indolently pacing along the pavement. After parking his vehicle, Rich remained motionless, looked around to make sure it was safe to proceed. He quietly spotted the colonel standing by an old wooden boat with its rusty metal anchor resting next to it. Yes, it was Andy Coleman, the author of the top-secret letter. Rich had served under the man in Iraq when he was a captain. Just under six foot tall, strong, solid arms, firm stomach, hard as a rock with muscles equal to any in the unit. Rich remembered when the captain had given him his staff sergeant rating and told him that he would be running a Black Operation unit in a few years. Reminiscing, Rich chastised himself for letting his guard down. He took a deep breath, looked around, and then, once again, was on full operational alertness.

As he walked toward Colonel Coleman, he could see his fingers pointing forward next to his left leg, and his right hand scratching his right ear. This gesturing was an old signal indicating someone was probably watching and listening. Once Rich approached the colonel, he swerved left to move around the aft of the old wooden sailboat. At this time, the colonel started walking away. As Rich rounded the aft on the starboard side, he spotted a comms unit sitting on a board. He pretended to tie his shoe, picked up the device, and kept walking in a different direction. As he sauntered across the street, he slipped the comms unit over his head and said, "I'm a go." Rich had not expected the response he heard.

"Very hot tomorrow. Meet me for an early breakfast, where we ate two years ago."

As Rich started to speak, there was static on the unit, and all he could make out were the letters CCC. In this poorly lit and eerie parking lot, the agent wondered if someone was watching him. Rich walked along the sidewalk bordering Maples street as the colonel drove away in his black government vehicle. Then, coming out of nowhere, he saw a second vehicle pulling out of the parking lot and following Colonel Coleman.

After walking for a while, Rich circled back to his car. As he leaned over to unlock the door, he heard a pop that sounded like a shot from a silencer, or when someone steps on an empty plastic water bottle. Still bent over, the agent pivoted toward the sound behind him and instantly brought his left arm up just as a hand armed with a knife was dropping down toward him. The lower part of Rich's arm hit the assailants ulna and radius just above the wrist. Almost at the same time, Rich brought his strong right fist up and forward, punching the man in the trachea. He heard his attacker suck for air as he dropped his knife, and brought both his hands to his throat. Rich kicked the man in his right leg just below the knee. The agent heard the cracking sound associated with a fracture. As the man fell to the ground, Rich picked up the knife and, with force, slammed it into the top of the man's head, the cranial injury caused a seizure. The man's arms and legs wiggled in all directions as he took his dying breath.

Rich opened the door of his rental car, left the lights off, and pulled onto Wharf Street. While adjusting his rearview mirror, he discovered someone was following him. Rich decided to enter the business district to lose his followers. Thoughts came back to the three letters he had heard on his comms unit. Gripping the staring wheel, he said, "CCC, what the hell does it mean?" While driving, his right hand-tested the comms unit resting on the passenger's seat; there did not seem to be anything wrong with it. Then he remembered he had grabbed his assailant's wallet. No time to look through it now, he thought. As he drove into the business area, Rich zigzagged, making right and left turns for close to twenty minutes before he finally ditched the black SUV that had been following him.

Sure he got rid of his stalkers; Rich drove back to the Avis car rental at the airport; he needed a different vehicle. After answering a few questions about the car's speedy return, the agent walked to the Hertz rental and left with a black Mercedes. Rich made numerous turns and used his training to make sure no one followed him on his way to his condo that had been left empty for quite a long time. Getting close to his apartment, the agent noticed the trees and plants around the building had grown during his absence. In the dark parking lot, he spotted a man across the street who seemed to be carrying something suspicious in his arms; something Rich could not identify. He felt like a fool as soon as he realized the older man was holding a small dog against his chest.

Rich found his door key hidden under a large rock, still sealed in its plastic bag. Before entering the condo, he looked for the hairs and paper he had glued on the doorknob a year ago; they were still there. Those little traps had for purpose to warn the homeowner of any breaking ins. After checking all the rooms in his home, he pulled out the return heating vent and extracted a bug-out kit containing a sniper rifle, a fold-up kind, and a SIG SAUER P229 with extra mags. There were many other items in the bag that an operator would need; he would have to take most of them. Rich pulled on a small rope and brought out another packet containing passports and twenty thousand dollars in cash. Once assured all was in place, Rich quickly showered and put on fresh black clothes. Feeling revived and ready to go, he locked the front door after placing the hairs and paperback on the doorknob. Once in his Mercedes, the agent took out his P229, chambered a round, and placed it in his left shoulder holster, with safety off. He grabbed three extra mags put them in holders on his belt. He instantly touched his right outer leg to make sure his razor-sharp knife was secure below his knee. Rich took out his driver's license bearing the name Richard Ferguson, his real name, which gave him access to government resources. He placed it in jacket left front pocket and took two-thousand dollars from his pack and transferred them to his right front pants pocket, along with two false replacement passports. He was ready.

Rich looked at his watch; it was just after four a.m. The letters CCC came to mind as he drove away from his condo, on his way to meet Colonel Coleman for an early breakfast. A little after five a.m., the agent parked at the Holiday Inn.

CHAPTER 3

A S HE GOT OUT OF HIS CAR, HE NOTED THE LIGHT overcast. Even though it was early in the morning, one could already feel the humidity. Inside the Washington-Capitol Holiday Inn deserted lobby, Rich glanced at his watch and noticed he was a few minutes late to meet with the colonel. As he entered the restaurant, Rich had no difficulty spotting Andy since he was the only guest in the dining room. He had selected a table next to an exit that had a window with a view. Rich observed Andy discreetly scratching his head to let him know it was safe to approach. In response, the agent touched his head once, a signal to indicate the message was received. Before Andy could greet him, Rich, still standing, said, "What the hell is the CCC? And why was I almost killed last night, right after you left?"

Looking puzzled, Colonel Coleman raised his eyebrows and grimaced. He had no idea someone had attacked Rich after his departure from the parking lot. The colonel started speaking, "You are not going to believe what has happened, son." The conversation stopped abruptly as the waitress was approaching their table. She set two cups and a large pot of coffee on their table and took their orders.

The colonel resumed, "So you can calm your nerves, let me start with the CCC. Let me tell you how I found out about this group and how it is out to put us six feet under."

Rich enjoyed a badly needed gulp of coffee. Even though he was eager to learn about the CCC, he was more interested in finding out who was behind the attack on him the night before. He took over the conversation and shared the incident, "After you left, someone tried to stab me in the back. I was lucky. I never saw the assassin, but I heard him as he approached me."

"What happened to him?"

"I stuck his knife in his forehead. Afterward, since I could not spot any cameras, I just left the body there, checked his wallet, and found a driver's license and a few hundred dollars." Rich reached into this pants pocket and brought out the leather wallet that he handed to the colonel. "I am sure this ID is as false as mine." Rich had nothing to add, "Please continue; I am anxious to know what is coming down." The colonel returned to the original subject, the CCC.

"Two weeks ago, I spoke with the President of the United States (POTUS). After stepping out of his office, I remembered I had left a folder there. I was just a few feet away. When I opened the door, I spotted someone standing in the President's office. I quietly grabbed the binder. Inadvertently, I left the door ajar, and as I was leaving, I heard the man speak inappropriately to POTUS. First, he addressed him by his first name. I slowed down, and I could hear the individual saying that the council was upset about the President's plans to bring troops back home from Afghanistan. After POTUS addressed that issue, this unknown man yelled that the council was pissed, and he accused the President of running a rogue outfit."

"Who in the hell was this visitor?"

"Hang on, son. After the man left the room, I closed the door and knocked. I told the President outright that I had heard part of the conversation. What I am going to say now is confidential." The waitress came by to offer more coffee. Colonel Coleman continued. "The CCC stands for Council Corporate Control. This group or committee was formed just before the Great Depression. Back then, the stock market was at an all-time high. The council knew there was very little money to be made from both the middle class and the more affluent individuals. Members of the CCC sold off all their stocks, took the profits, and caused the markets to crash. There was no more money to be made. After things got bad during the Great Depression, the CCC got together with President Franklin D. Roosevelt. They told him to come up with a solution to get more money flowing and to do this through federal programs that would relieve unemployment. President Roosevelt came up with a good idea to revive the country by creating, among other programs, the Civilian Conservation Corps. The CCC acronym of this public work relief program reminded the group of their power and what the council could do." After a few moments of silence, Rich said, "I still don't understand how a group of private citizens can tell POTUS what to do."

The colonel repositioned himself on his seat, looked around before he answered. "The CCC in question is made up of the filthy rich bankers from Europe and the United States, and it pretty much governs who can be elected. It does not matter if you are republican or democrat; they pull strings. Even most of the House and the Senate are under their control. They have the money to get whoever they want for President. With their political action committees (PACs), they pretty much control everything concocted in the White House. Even the Democratic Party has super PACs so they can control who they want as their nominee. It's almost impossible for a person to get elected without money, and the CCC controls the money. As soon as the new President is sworn in, representatives of the group meet with POTUS and present him with an outline of things he can and can't do. It also controls most of the actions of the Central Intelligence Agency (CIA) and the National Security Agency (NSA)." The colonel held up his hand so Rich would not interject. He took a long sip of his coffee and said, "Rich, the NSA is just an extension of the CCC."

Rich could not wait to humorously respond to the CIA acronym, "You mean the good old Christians In Action."

"Yes, that's them, many rich and some predominant members of the right and many rich and leading members of the Democratic party — the fornicators, God, Guns and Country, or money first. Before I forget, I should add that President Kennedy tried to do away with the CIA, and placed the office back under the OSI, run by the military. Look what happened to him."

"I have read a lot about his assassination, and it all points to the CIA, and very likely members of the New World Order, both were responsible for his death."

"You are right again, son. The CCC is behind the wars. As they say, the banks make more profit in a week with a war going than they get back with their lenders' interest in a year. The CIA sank our ship to justify the Vietnam War, just another example. The same happened with 911. The oil companies put President Bush in office, and the CCC selected Vice President Cheney. The CCC needed control of Iraq and Afghanistan after the Taliban had burned all the poppy fields, the source of funds for the CIA operations. Ghazni Province in Afghanistan may hold the world's largest lithium reserves. Those are three good reasons the CCC has put pressure on the presidents to keep our troops there."

"I know there is an oil pipeline going through Afghanistan." Rich was quick to reply.

"Right. The Oil Companies pipeline also runs into Pakistan. The recent Democratic President ran on the theme he would bring the troops home; well, elected and sworn in, he was taken aside by the CCC and told the troops would stay; in fact, he was ordered to send more troops. As I said, the CCC runs the country, and the President is only a figurehead." Then the colonel looked through the window; the morning sun was now almost at its peak and warming the swamp, city of big money and lobbyists. Andy looked at his watch; it was ten a.m. They had been talking for four hours. He turned around, took a sip of water, and said, "I am about to drown in urine, let's take a leak and go for a short walk. I have a lot more to tell you."

During the walk, the two men enjoyed the silence at first, and then Andy filled Rich in with many other details. It was after one p.m. when they returned to the Holiday Inn. After they ordered their lunch, the colonel continued his talk about the CCC. "Do you remember when I told you about the Bilderberger group and the Canada meeting several years ago?"

"Yes, I believe that was the year Mrs. Clinton was running for President."

"It sure was. It's speculated Clinton had gone to Canada to get the group's blessing to run for POTUS. However, the people voted in Obama; he had to submit to the will of the group. He surely knew what happened to John F. Kennedy and how they sent Nixon up for a fall when he ordered Nam's troops home. I have a folder for you here on the seat. All the information I have covered plus much more is in there. A representative of each member attends the Bilderberger meetings; these members have trained groups of killers who work for them, and they are used to control other members, leaders, etc. who get out of line or try to go up against the group. The CEO representative who came to the President's office is a man named Mr. Francois Lionel Campeau. He works for the Rothschild group, and from what I could find out from a geek friend of mine, he travels in the company of five killers, their leader is Pierre Paquet. He was a captain in the Legionnaires. I was able to find out that two of the other four are former Navy Seals who washed out of their unit. These are highly trained men, Rich." The colonel stared with insistence at Rich, hoping for a reaction.

"Do you want me to take out the leader?" One could detect concern in Rich's voice.

"Yes, but I assure you it will not be easy. You most likely will have to take out one or more of the hitmen to get to Francois Campeau. I am repeating it, son, do not take any chances. What POTUS and I want to do is send a warning to the group."

"What assistance and resources can I get?"

"Not much. I have a friend who can help you." Andy paused, took a long sip of hot coffee. "Here is the number you are to use to contact him, memorize it and discard it. Use a burner phone, and don't panic as the call will go through many connections around the globe before my friend answers. Here is an email address you can use as a last resort; once again, it will go through servers worldwide before getting to the right email user. The colonel wanted to make sure his instructions were clear. Then he said, "I have four burner phones for you. The number for each phone is on the back. After you leave a message, say 'number one,' and I will call you on the number two phone. POTUS and I hope you can interrogate Francois Campeau and find out who the other CCC men and women are, and obtain their locations. We want to eliminate as many as possible, but again, take no unnecessary chances." Colonel Coleman picked up the black folder lying on the seat next to him and handed it too Rich. "Memorize the information found inside and burn it, or hide it where no one will ever find it."

"What about your life, colonel; are you in any danger?"

"I don't think so as they do not know how much information I have on the group. Yes, they do follow me on occasions, but I am not worried yet since I am a presidential aide, any drastic action on their part would lead to an FBI investigation."

"Do you think they may be aware of your plan?"

"One of the NSA members is a mole. POTUS's office is swept for bugs every day, so it has to be someone protecting the President. I will set a few traps and see if we can narrow down the agents' shift first and then leave another trap to catch the culprit. Your job will be to eliminate the bastard when I find out who he is." There was silence for a few minutes. Andy tapped his fingertips on the table and said, "In the folder is the name of a contact you can use in Paris."

After finishing their lunch, the colonel informed Rich that he would use a rental box at the United Postal Service (UPS) store near the agent's condo, and Rich would be expected to check it every few days. It had been a long day. The two men gave each other a long hug and a slap on the back before heading for their vehicles.

CHAPTER 4

Rich watched the parking lot and the Holiday Inn's entrance for a while, ensuring no one followed the colonel. Assured of no suspicious presence, Rich pushed his front seat backward, opened the folder, and perused the CCC facts and information. He especially wanted to see the details provided regarding his hit on Mr. Pierre Paquet. While reading the report, the agent became enthralled and pissed at the same time. How could a group of CEOs and their masters run a democratic country like the United States? As time passed, he noted that the major chemical companies and the petroleum industry, along with the Rothschilds and other individuals, were members. As Rich kept on reading, he found out that banks in Europe, known billionaires, and even governors were also CCC members. The agent took his iPhone and typed 'Bilderberger group.' and discovered names of members probably active in the CCC. He could not possibly take out all those individuals, but if he could eliminate some of the big shots and the ones in charge of the dirty work, maybe the rest would realize that they are not invisible and are being watched. Rich read on for another half-hour before the cover page of his assignment came up.

He was to eliminate Pierre Paquet, a former legionnaire now employed by the Rothschilds, and as many of his select guards as possible. After turning the page, Rich found his address in Paris, France. He studied the photos of Pierre and the men working for him. He wrote their names on the back of the respective pictures and placed them in his pocket.

He perused the details concerning his assignment. At the top of the last page were the name, address, and phone number of his contact in Paris. Her name was Claire Laurent. The agent placed the information in the watch pocket of his pants. Then he moved to his second assignment.

He blinked several times as he read the name of John Hornbrook, a former Special Forces captain now working for an oil company in Texas. Oh, shit, he thought, the colonel is right, I might have taken on more than I can handle. Rich looked at the next assignment, which ordered him to go to the Ronald Reagan International airport and meet a man named Ralph Wiggins, a FedEx pilot. The agent was to give him the password listed, and the pilot would arrange for him to ride along in his cargo plane to Paris. Then came the last sentence, 'good luck, son.' Rich reread the last word, 'son,' a word with a happy connotation since he had been raised in foster homes and never knew his parents.

Now aware of his assignments, he started up the Mercedes and pulled out of the parking lot. After driving around a while to assure himself no one was following him, he headed back to his condo to pick up a few items he might need in Paris. It took him an hour to reach his apartment.

He noted that his invisible little traps, the hairs, and small piece of paper were missing from his front door. Someone had tampered with it. He moved around the side of his unit with his Sig Sauer in hand, loaded and ready. Looking through the windows, he could see no one in any of the rooms. Before opening the front door, a bit apprehensive, he thought about the possibility that a bomb could go off upon entering. Taking no chance, he pulled off the screen to his sliding door, then successfully worked the hatch. With his silencer screwed on his gun, he vigilantly checked each room; there was no one inside the apartment. The agent checked his drawers to see if the strategically placed hairs were still there; they were not. Someone had gone meticulously through his condo, careful not to leave any evidence behind.

The agent selected a change of clothes and gathered items he needed to take along. After a long hot shower, followed by twenty seconds of cold water, he put on clean clothes, checked his pack, and moved toward his front door. A bit hesitant, Rich opened the door, placed the hairs and a small piece of paper back on the doorknob. He was on his way to the airport from which he would fly to Paris.

The sun had set, and the city lights glowed throughout the city. Two hours later, he met up with Captain Ralph Wiggins, the pilot. After giving him the code, Wiggins told him that they would be flying out at midnight. Ralph gave Rich a set of brown coveralls with a FedEx symbol across the back. "You will need to wear these to get close to the plane." Ralph gave Rich a few more instructions and left.

CHAPTER 5
Paris

WITH HIS COAT PULLED TIGHT AROUND HIM, RICH was sleeping when Captain Ralph left the cockpit to talk to him. The pilot waited a moment, then Ralph tapped Rich on the shoulder, "You must have been tired to sleep so long on that horrible chair."

"I have had very little sleep for the past two days."

Ralph handed Rich a cup with a FedEx symbol printed on it. Rich smiled as he saw the steaming hot coffee. "Maybe this will help wake you up." Ralph watched Rich sip the coffee. He added, "We will be landing in Paris at the Le Bourget Airport in about thirty minutes. The door is unlocked if you need to wash up."

"Thanks, cap. What's the procedure to get through the terminal."

"Put your brown FedEx coveralls back on. Just follow me, they never check the crew of the cargo planes. Once through the gate, you are on your own. Here is my cell phone number in case you need a ride home. Hide the paper, better yet, memorize the number and throw away the note."

"Thanks. I hope our mutual friend takes good care of you."

"He does, and I would do it for nothing as he saved my life a long time ago. I love Colonel Coleman like a brother. Buckle up; we will be landing soon." Rich savored his coffee, and Ralph went back into the cockpit.

Preparing to disembark, the agent pushed his legs through the one-piece brown FedEx suit. He pulled the pants up over his own, stuck his arms in the oversized sleeves, and, once ready, buttoned the coveralls halfway up and sat back down to wait for the landing. Within ten minutes, he heard the usual grind of the landing gear, then felt the bounce before the plane began to brake.

With his bags over his shoulder, Rich followed Ralph through the loading dock area where he got his passport stamped before walking to the car rental area.

After signing the paperwork under the name Matt Williamson, Rich walked out to the lot to retrieve a black Mercedes. He instinctively looked under and around the vehicle for possible bombs before opening the door of the car. Satisfied, he opened the front door, threw his bag on the back seat, and removed his FedEx heavy suit before getting in. Rich started the German precision vehicle. While the car was warming up, he programmed his GPS to go to the Paris Marriott Champs-Élysées Hotel at 70 Avenue des Champs-Élysées. While in flight, he had reserved a room there under the name of Matt Williamson, the same name he had used upon his arrival back in Washington DC. The CCC was aware of his car rental under the name of Matt Williamson in Washington. As soon as this name popped up on the computer of Pierre Paquet's office in Paris, a scheme to entice the agent to report to a given location was in the planning.

Rich followed the route suggested on the screen in the Mercedes. Although he had to remain vigilant, Rich could not help noticing the sun's hue glowing off the City of Light's mansard roofs and old stone buildings. It was early morning; people were walking and driving to work. Because the traffic was so dense at times, Rich felt unnerved. Driving in Paris is a challenge, and this explains why thirty-eight percent of Parisians do not own a car. Public transportation, subway, buses, and taxi cabs are readily available. Also, Paris is the most walkable city in the world.

Finally, he pulled into the darkened area of the parking lot of the Marriott. After checking in the vehicle, Rich wandered toward the dining area of the hotel. He was hungry and tired from the long flight spent on an uncomfortable seating arrangement. The smell of fresh-baked bread and croissants was overwhelming. As Rich was sipping his hot cup of coffee, a lady, maybe five foot nine or ten sauntered toward his roundtable.

She had on a short black skirt, a violet blouse opened in front, giving a view of her pronounced breasts. Her hair was loose, naturally flowing, and she wore very little makeup, just a touch of light red to her full lips. As she placed her right hand on the chair close to Rich's, he noticed her black five-inch spike heels, which, when she walked, gave her body a sexy look. Rich immediately presumed that she was a lady of the night working overtime.

Without any hesitation, and without consulting Rich, she pulled the chair next to his and sat down. Her legs were magnificent, and her way of crossing them enhanced their firmness. She ordered a cup of cafe au lait and turned to Rich, who had remained silent and a bit surprised by this unexpected company. With a smile and unexpected familiarity, she addressed Rich, "You from around here, honey, or just passing through?" she asked.

The woman he thought resembled a lady he had dated before, but when she spoke, there was no resemblance to his soft-spoken girlfriend. Rich was in no mood to make conversation, so he was brief with his reply, "Business." The woman felt his rejection, but insisted,

"I was trying to make conversation, dear. Again, are you from around here?"

"I am in town on business."

"Are you here for a conference?"

Rich looked at her this time. He did not want to get dragged into a dialogue. The woman realized her company was not wanted, she looked at Rich and asked,

"Do you mind if I sit here?"

"No problem, I am going to have breakfast. May I order you something?"

"Just coffee, thanks. My name is Mia."

"My name is Matt, and I am from New York."

"I lived in the Washington DC area for several years," Mia replied softly.

Rich looked at her with surprise and said, "Have you ever eaten at Captain Jack's seafood restaurant on 5th street?"

"Oh yes, probably a couple of times. Good food and excellent ambiance."

Rich wondered if he was being set up. He decided to follow along to see where Mia led him.

Mia pulled her skirt up just a little, leaned over so Rich could see the delicate black lace of her slip, and whispered, "Do you have any cocaine?"

Rich shook his head and raised his voice and enunciated, "I don't touch drugs."

"I wish I had never started; I am hooked. What are you doing for the rest of the day?"

"I have nothing planned. I need to clean up after I finish eating."

Mia looked around and leaned toward Rich. Rich could smell the Chanel number five she was wearing. "I have something in mind you might enjoy. Some friends of mine are having a party. I am inviting you. Would you like to go?"

Rich did not respond immediately. Mia had lied twice already. Then he said, "I don't like parties much."

"Me neither, but I like to drink, and I am sure you also do. There will be lots of men there, and plenty of booze, what do you think?"

"OK. But first let me go take a shower, change clothes and I will meet you there in thirty minutes." After Mia agreed to wait for him, Rich went to his room, took a quick shower, and changed into his only spare shirt. The agent had no idea what he was getting into, so he screwed the silencer onto his gun, secured his seal knife to his leg, and his short sword, as he called it, to his belt behind his back. Rich was now ready to party, one way or another.

Rich returned to the dining room, and sure enough, Mia was still sitting at the table. "Let's head for the parking lot and pick up my car." As they approached his Mercedes, Rich said, "You are going to drive since you know your way around Paris.

Mia was all smiles as she opened the driver's side door and laughed as she slid in behind the steering wheel. She started the engine of the big German-made vehicle and pulled out onto the street. "You are going to love this party."

Suddenly the atmosphere in the car changed. Rich reached under his left shoulder and pulled out his Sig Sauer with the silencer attached, and swiftly placed the barrel against Mia's head. "I don't like parties, and you are a liar. I am going to get the truth out of you one way or another."

The car veered a little as Mia froze. She was so shocked that she was stuttering when she said, "Please, don't hurt me. I was paid to ask you to come to that party."

CHAPTER 6

M IA WAS SHAKING, CAUSING THE CAR TO SWERVE AS she drove down the Champs-Elysees. With tears rolling on her cheeks, she said, "Why are you doing this? Why are you putting that gun to my head?"

"You are a liar, and I know what you are doing, you are setting me up. Just drive to wherever you were told to take me."

"The people who hired me never said there would be a gun, and anything bad would happen." More tears were leaving black mascara lines on her face. Rich knew that she was bait.

He wondered how the CCC had found out he was in Paris and how they had located him. He realized he had made a mistake using the same name in Paris that he had put on the rental car application in DC. Then Rich let his thoughts return to the present. He knew why the CCC had hired Mia, a beautiful woman, well dressed, and naive, who would not intimidate their target or raise suspicion. But her lies and her nervousness gave her away. Rich was sure she was hired to lead him to his death or capture to obtain information. He had to change the game plan. During the drive, the agent had lowered his gun. Mia required full concentration to cope with heavy traffic. The sniffling having decreased, he brought the gun back against her temple.

Tears were flowing again, and the whining resumed. "Don't kill me, please. I will help you in any way I can. I have done nothing wrong. Some man offered me two thousand euros to bring you to the people who hired me. I swear that is all that I was asked to do."

"What is your real fucking name, Mia?"

"Nicole Couture, but I use Mia when I am working. I took this job because I needed the money, and no one said I would be in danger." So much pressure while driving in heavy traffic with a gun brushing her temple caused Mia to hyperventilate. "I—I didn't think anyone would get hurt. Please, please, just let me go."

"Are you acting? Better wise up."

"No, I swear. I am scared. Please, stop and let me go."

"You are going to take me to this so-called party. "Rich pulled the gun away from Mia's head and said, with an authoritative voice, "Take the car within half a block of the party, then stop and point out the exact location. When we get there, I will tell you what to do next." Already Rich was regaining his calm. He was on the offensive and was calling the shots. Five minutes later, Mia pulled up and parked in a narrow alley littered with debris, papers, plastic bottles, and cans. It was evident to Rich this was an industrial section of the city where warehouses lined the streets, and no homes could be found. Mia informed Rich that the party was taking place in a white one-story building on the right side of the road. She told him that on the front double door, he would find a handwritten sign reading 'Soiree Privee' (Private Party).

"Is there a back door or a side door where I can gain access?"

Mia had stopped crying, but she was still nervous when she answered, "There is a door in the back which opens on an alley. In the alley, against the building, there is a metallic ladder that runs to the roof."

"To be sure you don't play further tricks on me, I will tie you up and leave you in the trunk. If I get out of this mess alive, I will turn you loose and give you one-thousand euros. If you scream while in the trunk or give me any problems, I will kill you. Do you understand?"

The tears flowed again as Mia spoke, "I understand, I promise I will remain quiet."

Considering the uncertain outcome of the situation, Mia added, "May I have the money now in case you don't come back?"

"Do you take me for a fool. You were willing to take me to a trap to get killed, and now you want favors." Stunned by her daring attitude, Rich looked at Mia with his eyes narrowed, and his lips pressed together, saying, "You are lucky I don't just kill you and drop your body in the Seine river." Mia parked about half a block from the white building.

The deserted dark alley provided cover. Rich tied a docile Mia up, placed a gag in her mouth, and gently dropped her in the Mercedes trunk. He checked his arms, left the alley, and worked his way to the street on foot. He needed to get a layout of the buildings and see how many cars were parked along the sidewalk. The area appeared inhabited, almost abandoned. A few yards away, he spotted a man who was smoking a cigarette. Rich took out the pictures that Andy had given him. He looked through the five small photos he was carrying in his pocket and identified the stalking man. The individual was a former Navy Seal that had washed out of the service for drunkenness. His name was Sergeant Ronald P. Jorgenson. Rich studied the area around where the man was standing. He wondered if he should climb the exit stairs of the adjoining building, go over the roof and shoot the sergeant from the top of the building. His only other choice was to confront the man head-on.

Rich reached into his pocket, brought out the silencer, and screwed it on his Sig. After serious consideration, he decided to climb the old wrought iron ladder up to the roof. Very slowly moving up the shale shingles to the top of the building, he worked his way along the edge of the structure. The street was free of pedestrians; there was no one in sight, except Jorgenson. The coast was clear. Rich pulled the Sig Sauer with the silencer on it, aimed, fired, and hit the man just above the right ear. Without a sound, the victim collapsed to his knees, then fell sideways. To make sure there was no chance he would survive, Rich put a second round into his head and looked around to make sure no one had seen what had just happened. He climbed down the shaky wrought iron steps, which seemed to be hanging by only a few screws stuck into the granite. Before stepping off, Rich gave a circular look at the surroundings. All he could see were Gitane cigarette butts, a few old empty wine bottles, and fast food wrappers here and there. The agent grabbed the body and dragged it to the alley's end, where stood a large dumpster. The agent accidentally ripped the dead man's shirt and was somewhat surprised to see that Jorgenson was wearing the newest model of body armor issued by the US military. It was a lucky break that he shot the guard in the head. A bullet would not have dented this armor. In a hurry, he removed the body protection and put it on under his leather jacket. Rich removed the man's wallet, took out the euro notes, and put them in his front pants pocket along with the car keys and passport. Rich wanted the crime to look like a robbery. The agent took a picture of the dead man with his phone to send it to the colonel. Rich then reached for the man's money belt. Inside it, rolled tightly, were over two thousand euros that he placed in his right pocket with the other notes. With difficulty, Rich lifted the body onto the edge of the dumpster, then, with force, pushed it over the side. When he heard Jorgenson hit the metal bottom of the empty trash container, he smiled and said, "More trash." Rich collected an old newspaper and a few grocery plastic bags littering the passageway and threw them over the corpse.

Once more, he looked down both ends of the back alley. Spotting no one, he decided to move with caution to the opposite side of the building. Rich was sure that Pierre Paquet, the security chief, would be there and probably have at least one of his five men present. That meant there were most likely only two individuals inside the building. Rich took his time to check out thoroughly the structure from different angles. He needed to get inside the premises. What was critical and made Rich's entrance inside dangerous was that he had no idea of the floor plan or the number of guards present.

He moved back to a small boarded up window he had spotted earlier. He tried to look through the dirty glass after attempting to wipe it clean with his handkerchief; this was a useless effort. As he was scraping the filth from the window, one of the old boards came loose. As quietly as he could, he pulled the board off so it would not fall on the floor noisily and attract attention. Next came a second, and a third board covering the only source of light in the room. Rich studied the old casement window with four of the eight panes missing, removed the rest of them along with the mastic, the crumbling puttylike sealer, that held them in place. Once the agent was sure the opening was wide enough, he gave a final look around the alley. With his gun in one hand, he slid through the small opening with difficulty; his jacket was getting caught in the window frame's uneven and sharp edges. Rich was now inside a semi-dark room. Adjusting to the lack of light, he listened for voices. Faintly the agent could pick up someone speaking. Then he heard a second voice.

Rich moved like a mouse toward the sound and put his ear to the wall. "They are late, they should be here, stay by the door so when the woman comes in, you take charge and keep him covered."

"Roger that cap."

Rich was desperately looking for a peephole, a fissure, just a small opening to get a good look at those individuals behind the wall. Inside the small room, Rich found a door with a keyhole plugged with dust, dirt, cobwebs, but no key. He bent over and held his mouth against the filthy lock and gave several puffs of air. Through the keyhole, he could hardly make out one of the two men, which, according to the picture, he pulled out of his pocket, was Captain John Hornbrook. Then the agent was able to see Timothy

Smithwright, a former sergeant in the Green Berets. The CCC sure knows how to get the best talents, Rich thought to himself. He had to plan his next move, which was to face the two men. Rich figured the door which had no knob or handle could be forced open.

CHAPTER 7

Rich thought about the situation for several minutes. Standing motionless, the agent studied the door by gingerly pushing it at different levels. There was resistance. He pulled it inward by sliding his fingers underneath the narrow gap at the base of the door. He carefully inched the door open the width of a finger. Now, he could see both men. Tim was standing to the right of the front door, and his boss, John, former special forces captain, was to Rich's left, sitting in a chair against the wall. Since neither man had a weapon in his hand, the best action was to take the fight directly to them. He would barge into the room with the dead sergeant's gun in one hand, and his own in the other. If either one moved a muscle, he would shoot first then ask questions.

The door was now slightly ajar. The agent grabbed the panel and, in a split second, violently opened the door. Rich pointed Jorgensen's gun at each man, and said, "Don't move a muscle, or even speak, until I tell you, or you're dead." The element of surprise was so impressive that for a second, the two men found themselves in an unresponsive stupor from which they recovered almost immediately.

Ignoring the order, and without hesitation, Tim furtively moved his right arm under his jacket to grab his gun. Without any explanation, Rich shot him in his right leg, Tim dropped his weapon. "I said, don't move. Now, Mr. Timothy, I want you to drag yourself slowly toward Mr. Hornbrook." Rich had figured that using the title, would puzzle and maybe intimidate the two men. "If you even blink Mr. Hornbrook, I will shoot you; do you copy?"

The response was quick to follow, "Fuck you, Richard. I don't know how you figured things out, but you are a dead man."

Rich said, "Your girlfriend gave herself away. Now we are going to have a little talk. Don't worry about your friend Jorgensen. He is sleeping peacefully at the bottom of a dumpster. Tim, you sit in that chair just to the right of Mr. Hornbrook. I will ask questions only once. If I get no answer, someone suffers. Do you understand?"

Rich heard the insults that followed. He ordered John to take his weapon out with two fingers and throw it on the floor."

"Fuck you asshole, come and get it."

A single shot rang out, and John grabbed his left knee with both his hands, whining in pain. "One more time, take two fingers and pull out your weapon." Grimacing in pain, John pulled his weapon out from under his left shoulder and dropped it on the floor, at his feet. "Kick it away from you with your good leg."

With disdain, John said, "Fuck you," as he kicked the weapon away. He added, "What the fuck do you want, asshole?"

"Same as you, information. Where is Pierre Paquet, your boss?"

"Look it up in the white pages fucker," Tim yelled.

Without hesitation, Rich shot Tim in the left knee. As the man held his knee and screamed in pain, Rich added, "One more time, the address of Pierre Paquet."

John almost screamed out the address. "You spoke too fast, Mr. John," Rich said. "I am going to approach you with Mr. Pierre Paquet's picture. I want you to write his address on the back. Either of you makes a move, and you're dead." John had tears running down his cheeks, and he was shaking as he wrote the address. Then he slowly handed it too Rich. After Rich picked up John's gun, he walked over to Tim and said, "You write the address on the back of your picture, if it does not match Hornbook's, you are dead."

"I, I, I am sure he never gave you the right address. Let me write it for you."

"You son of a bitch, you are selling me out. Fuck both of you, as for you asshole, you are a dead man."

"Write the address. I already have it anyway, but I want to see if yours matches mine. Also, I wanted to see if either of you was truthful." As Rich watched, Tim wrote an address on the back of his picture and handed it too Rich. "It looks like the only liar we have here is you, Mr. Hornbrook." Rich then shot Hornbrook in the head.

"What about me, sir, I gave you the right address."

"I know that, but you were going to kill me; is that right?"

"No, no, we were just going to interrogate you."

Without hesitation, Rich shot the man in the head. Rich then put John's weapon in Tim's hand and fired a shot using Tim's finger. For the investigators, it would look like Tim had shot John. Then Rich walked up to the former special forces captain and placed Tim's gun in his hand, and using the dead man's finger, fired a shot. Blood and brain matter splattered on the floor. Rich reached behind his back and placed Sergeant Ronald Jorgenson's gun in his holster, and his two mags in his pocket. Before leaving the building, Rich removed the dead men's money and wallets, then took a picture of each of the deceased to send to the colonel. Rich left the building the way he had entered, then worked his way back toward the Mercedes.

He tapped on the Mercedes trunk lid, made sure no one was in earshot, and said, "I will drive around for a while, then I will let you sit up front. Kick the metal if you heard me." After he heard a faint sound, Rich slowly drove down the street. It was not long before he found an out of the way alley. After parking, Rich opened the trunk, reached in and removed the tape covering Mia's mouth. As she started to speak, Rich told her to whisper. He removed the tape around her wrists and legs. "Come and get upfront with me, I have something to tell you."

Rich looked at Mia. He felt sorry for the woman. "I'm so dehydrated, I need water," Mia said as she wiped her brows.

Rich turned toward the rear seat and picked up a plastic bottle of Evian spring water. "How much of the two thousand euros did your friends pay you already."

Almost choking, Mia said, "One, one thousand euros. I was to get the rest after you walked into the building."

"Just a minute." He then pulled out the wallet taken from Jorgenson. It was thick with euros. Rich knew the assassins intended to kill her and keep her money. Rich took the thick wad of euro notes from the wallet. He counted out two-thousand in euros that he handed to Mia, who immediately hid them away in her pocket.

"Thanks, thank you. I am so sorry if I got you in trouble."

Rich threw her empty bottle in the back seat and placed the remaining euros in the bottle holder between the two seats. "At the end of the street, I see a boulangerie (bakery), go get us a couple of sandwiches and some cold water. I will wait for you here."

Mia reached on the floor of the passenger side to recover her purse. She combed her hair the best she could, put on a dash of makeup, just a little bit of color on her lips. "Please, be here when I come back." She put on the best smile she could as she opened the car door and stepped outside.

"I will be here." In her absence, Rich took out all of the euros from each wallet and counted them. "Holy shit," he said out loud. Then he gathered the money from the other two men; the booty totaled over eight-thousand euros. Rich took the money and placed it inside his jacket.

Mia looked refreshed as she walked up to Rich's side of the car. "Here is a ham and cheese sandwich and a large cold bottle of Vichy water." Then she walked around the front of the vehicle and got in the passenger side. "I was sure you would leave while I was gone. How come you never left?" Her eyes looked worried; she was concerned as she waited for a reply.

"I don't treat women like that, especially not one who has been exploited and even abused. Let's eat; then I will take you back to the hotel where we met."

Another hour had passed before Rich drove into the parking lot at the Paris Marriott. "Before we say goodbye, you may have the money rolled up in the bottle holder."

A few tears appeared on Mia's cheek, then she said, "You do not have to do that. Please forgive me." As she shyly reached for the money, she moved over close to Rich. She looked at him in the eyes, then leaned forward and kissed him on each cheek. "You do not know it, but this money will help me." Mia stepped out of the Mercedes and shut the door.

Rich left the Marriott hotel for good as the CCC had found him once, and he would not make the same mistake again.

CHAPTER 8

AFTER RETURNING THE MERCEDES TO THE CAR RENTAL, Rich walked around the airport looking for a different rental agency. Using an altered passport and driver's license, he selected a 3008 Peugeot SUV. After completing the paperwork, the agent took time off to sit down at a small airport restaurant for a coffee cup. Following the execution of John, Tim, and Jergerson, Rich realized that the other members of the team of assassins he was expected to eliminate would be on the defensive. He knew it was going to be a challenge to take out Paquet and Smithwright.

To make matters worse, Rich was aware the two men were protected by well-trained security personnel. While lazily enjoying his coffee, Rich perused information about the Rothschild family on Wikimedia. He could not believe the power, wealth, and control the family had over other people in different parts of the world. Rich looked at the file that Andy had given him. He could not find the Rothschilds' address in Paris but had Paquet's, the security guru, or headhunter for the CCC. The agent remembered that Andy had told him to call Marguerite Boucher in Paris for help. He plugged Marguerite's phone number into his secure government phone. The agent had mentally prepared what he would say to this professional contact he had never met. It was not until after the fifth ring that he heard someone breathing into the mike. Rich thought for a moment then uttered the code, "Paris is not always light."

Rich waited, hoping to hear the words, "Neither is DC." Then softly, someone said, "Neither is DC." The voice sounded young. With a sigh of relief, Rich replied, "I need your help, where can we meet?" "Are you at the airport or in the city?"

"I just rented a vehicle here at Le Bourget airport. I can meet you anywhere in the city."

"Meet me in two hours at the Le petit sandwich, a small cafe about two blocks from the park entrance, 3 Rue des Victoires. I assume you have a GPS."

"I do. I will see you there in about two hours, depending on the traffic."

"When you get there, go to a table for two. When the waitress comes to your table, order, a cup of coffee, a croissant, and a Pernod, that unusual combination will help me identify you." The connection went dead.

What the hell is a Pernod, Rich thought? Once in his vehicle, he programmed the address in the car's GPS. Fortunately, the Peugeot had an English translation of the verbal directions. Rich reached Boulogne Park and spotted the meeting place right away. After fifteen minutes, he finally found a parking lot. As he approached the cafe, he noticed it was surrounded by planters from which pink ivy geraniums were cascading. A few clients were present on the front terrace. No one paid attention to him. He entered the building where a small group of patrons was enjoying pastries, and again, no one noticed him. The waitress approached Rich immediately. As suggested by his Paris contact, he ordered a croissant, a coffee, and a Pernod. He had no idea what that last item was, food or drink. It was delivered along with a small carafe of cold water. Rich figured he was to add the water to the one-inch brilliant and clear yellow spirit at the bottom of the tall glass. Immediately the transparent spirit turned milky-opaque. The drink tasted like licorice.

A svelte woman entered the room; she was short but well proportioned, blond with blue eyes. She immediately noticed Rich, waved at him, and joined him. The agent got up to shake her hand, but instead, she kissed him on both cheeks to give the world an impression of mutual familiarity between her and a regular customer. He knew, of course, that this display of friendship was part of the game. After very brief introductions, the young woman said jokingly, "We usually do not drink Pernod until evening, monsieur."

Rich was not expecting a black ops operator, spy, or whatever her title, to look like this woman, so small, cute and petite. She did not look anything like the daughter of the picture that Andy had provided. When she returned with a glass of water, Rich mentioned the lack of resemblance between her and the photo he had of her. She explained, "That photo is the wrong agent. It was sent to protect me, I am your assigned agent." Intrigued by the reply, Rich would call Andy later to confirm this unexpected substitution.

Rich took a few more sips of his Pernod, which he found refreshing and exotic. Their conversation remained superficial and brief. This meeting was to meet Rich and arrange for a more secluded setting to discuss business.

Now sitting at the table, she went over a few basics, "I will be your contact. After you leave, I will meet you down the street near your car." Rich was puzzled. How did she know where he had parked his car?

The agent finished his Pernod for which he had acquired a taste. Leaving the cafe, he looked around, hoping to spot Sabine. He was almost back to his vehicle when he saw her step out of a side street. She said, "The CCC has eyes and ears in high places, and I wanted to make sure you had not been followed. Let's sit in your car and talk. Rich spoke first.

"I need your help to find the head of a security group that works for the Rothchilds. The man I am after is Pierre Paquet, if that is his real name." Sabine knew of Paquet.

"That individual and those who work with him are very evil and extremely dangerous. I know where his office is; not far from here, that is why I chose to meet you here. As you may know, your boss, Mr. Coleman, asked me to help you. Others like you, and I, want this man dead. These people have no scruples and are very greedy. Let me drive, and I will take you by an old mansion so you can see where the Rothchilds lodge some of their guards."

Five minutes later, they slowly drove by a large house covered with ivy and surrounded by a front-yard full of unkempt vegetation. Rich said, "It seems to be run down."

"Yes, it is terribly neglected. There is an office inside a garage in the back. This annex is Paquet's headquarters. It does not look like much, so it does not attract attention.

The mansion can accommodate many guards. Did you spot any as I drove by the building?"

"No, but I saw cameras on the corners of the roof. And it's tough for me to believe this garage would be Pierre's office."

"It is one of many. Usually, when not here, Pierre is not far. There are cameras in the trees, motion alarms in and around the old garage. It will be challenging to attack Pierre at this location."

"Drive around one more time; I might have an idea." Rich studied the residence and could not understand why a family worth over a half-trillion dollars, or more, would let such a beautiful and imposing old structure fall apart. As Sabine finished the loop around the site, he said, "Let's go somewhere and park; I think I have figured a way to get in."

After purchasing coffee, they sat quietly under some trees. Rich ran several ideas through his mind. Then he said, "I will not make a conventional entry inside the house. I will be going over the roof and drop down onto the top of the garage. That is the only safe way I can think of to get in."

"Are you crazy? The building is very high, I-I am afraid of heights."

"Don't worry, I work alone, but I will need you to create a diversion." Also, I am going to write a list of things I need you to get for me." As Rich wrote down the items he wanted, he explained the significant role that Sabine would play. He laid his pen down and said, "We must have two comms units. Do you think we can find all of the items by tomorrow?"

Sabine looked at the list. "Some of these items will cost you extra, it is such short notice, but yes, I think I can get what you want. I will take you with me, be at the cafe at eight a.m. Now you can go back to study the building." He took her back to the cafe where they had met. Without a word, she left and headed down the street.

Back at the Rothchild's mansion, the area was quiet. He pulled out his binoculars. Throughout the remainder of the day, Rich scrutinized the old building until the sun began to set. Several times, at regular intervals, he observed a guard come out and go around the structure. Once satisfied with his observations, the agent returned to his hotel.

CHAPTER 9

RICH SHOWERED, ATE DINNER, AND WALKED THE streets until close to midnight. He was restless. He never paid much attention to the charm and the beauty of the city of light at night. The agent was bothered that a woman would be physically assisting him in such a dangerous op. It was way past midnight when fatigue overcame him.

The next day, he ate breakfast early, took a walk before daylight, and drove to meet Sabine. She asked to sit in the driver's seat and said, "I will drive. You keep an eye on the road. I am taking you to Saint-Denis, also known as the '93'. 93 is the number of the 'department' of Seine-Saint-Denis, an administrative division within a region called Ile-de-France. The country is divided into 96' departments.' This one is located in the north-east of Paris, some thirty kilometers from here. It has a large migrant population. Because of a few troublemakers, mostly migrants or children of migrants, who have never been able to integrate well into the mainstream of French society, this city has acquired a bad reputation. I have a dependable contact in Saint-Denis, he has most of the supplies you need.

The sun glistened off buildings as they drove toward their destination. People were running here and there like they did not know where they were going. Suddenly, Sabine turned into a narrow street and slowly drove to the end of the cul-de-sac. As she got out of the car, she whispered, "You stay here. I'll be back in about ten minutes."

It was closer to twenty minutes before his partner returned with a large khaki duffle bag. As she slid into the front seat, she said, "My friend had all the stuff we need. Now, we have to go to another contact of mine to get the comms units. He has them in stock."

Rich thanked her. While on the road, he shared with Sabine what had been on his mind ever since he met her. "I did not expect a young woman to be assigned to me, and I don't know if you have been warned how dangerous this mission is."

Looking stern, Sabine turned toward him and said, "I have been in contact with Colonel Coleman, I am fully informed, and ready to follow your orders." Rich did not pursue; instead, he returned to details concerning the assignment. "Are there a lot of gendarmes cruising in the vicinity of the mansion during the day?"

"It is a low crime neighborhood. The police are seldom seen in this sector. With good silencers on our weapons, I suggest we attack early in the morning, around six a.m. If you want to go early tomorrow, I am ready. Thinking, Rich rolled his lips on top of each other several times. He agreed, "Let's do it tomorrow, early."

They made another stop. Sabine left again and was back in the car in less than ten minutes. She stuck her head through the window, handed Rich the two comms units, and said, "It will cost you one thousand euros. As you know, money can do most anything in any country. Remember, cash buys silence." Rich decided to quit for the day and suggested she drop him at his hotel, "Do you mind taking me to my hotel? You can keep the car and pick me up in the morning."

"No. Take me back to the cafe. Meet me back there no later than five a.m tomorrow. Before we separate, we should go back to the mansion one more time and do a final recon." Rich said, "I did a good recon yesterday, and I can do another one after I drop you. But since you insist, it would be better for the two of us to do this last recon together on foot. There is a park not far from the mansion. Let's go park there, and this time, walk around the neighborhood."

Following their purposeful stroll in the quiet streets, Rich invited his partner to lunch. To his surprise, Sabine accepted the invitation. At the restaurant, to make things simple for Rich, who could not read the menu, she selected something she enjoyed for the both of them, boeuf bourguignon. This standard of French cuisine consists of beef braised or stewed in a red wine sauce, to which mushrooms and onions are typically added. Sabine could not help quote the well known American chef, Julia Child, who described the dish as "certainly one of the most delicious beef dishes concocted by man." Rich agreed, the stew was delicious.

After dropping Sabine, Rich headed back to the hotel.

CHAPTER 10

FTER AN AGITATED NIGHT, THE AGENT DECIDED TO JOG several blocks. He was now slowing his pace to lower his heart rate. Back in his room, he worked out on the floor before showering. It was 4:00 a.m., time to get ready.

As coffee was brewing in his room, the agent put on a new black polo shirt and a dark Levi pair of pants. Sitting on the edge of the bed, he cleaned his Sig, screwed on the silencer, and placed three extra mags in his belt holders. While finishing his first coffee cup, he attached his two knives, one below the knee, and a short one behind his back. Rich then packed a small number of personal things he had brought with him in his pack. He placed his passport and driver's license inside his leather jacket, checked both documents to make sure they were the right ones, and the names were identical. Except for breakfast, Rich was ready. He headed for his Peugeot. Driving down the Champs-Elysées and around the Arc de Triomphe, the city appeared strangely silent and deserted. Even though the sun had not risen yet, the town was now starting to come alive. Street cleaners, garbage collectors, and suppliers moved silently like rats to deliver the fresh goods to their vendors and collect the waste a large city produces each day. Another twenty minutes passed before Rich pulled across the cafe, which was closed at this early time, except for Rich.

As he walked in, he noticed Sabine was alone in her mom's business. She was wearing a white apron wrapped around her tiny waist and had on a pair of jeans. Her hair was tied in a bun behind her head. She walked up to him and said, "I have a table over there, sir," and pointed toward the little round table where he had sat before. "Would you like a couple of fresh croissants with your coffee?"

Rich could see the tiredness in Sabine's eyes, but yet they sparkled like diamonds, and she was moving with vitality. It was only a few minutes before she returned with a small pot filled with fragrant coffee and a couple of warm and golden croissants. Sabine bent over and said, "I am almost ready, take your time. When finished, return to your vehicle. I will meet you there."

As usual, Rich was eating too fast. He took a breath and slowed down to enjoy the light and rich buttery, flaky, crispy croissants, a delicate taste he had not experienced in the military. Sabine had disappeared. As she had instructed him earlier, he returned to his car. Almost immediately, his partner came up from behind his vehicle and tapped on the trunk. Sabine said, "I will drive where we have our supplies stored. We have less than one hour before sunrise." The ride to the arms cache was short. In silence, the agents transferred the equipment needed for their assault. Then Sabine handed Rich a small bottle and said, "Here is the chloroform."

Rich pulled the two bulletproof vests from the back seat, handed one to his partner, and ordered her to put it on. Then they tested the comms units. Rich said, "Here's the final plan. I will go over the back end of the mansion using a rope and hook. I will lower myself to the ground in the front of the and use chloroform to put any guards down that crosses my way. If not feasible, we will have to put them down in a more permanent way."

Sabine was concerned; she still did not know what part she would play. "What exactly do you want me to do?"

Do you know how to use that gun you are holding?" He knew she could. He had reached Andy the night before to review a few things about his new partner. The colonel had reassured the agent concerning Sabine's competence. Rich, who had never worked closely with women in covert operations where danger was real had to adjust to the new partnership. After all, she had been assigned to him by Colonel Coleman, a wise man whom he trusted.

"I was taught how to shoot years ago by my mother, who was taught by your colonel." Rich asked, "Do you mean Colonel Coleman? I am a bit puzzled now." Sabine clarified things for her partner, "My mother was assigned to the Balkans during the conflict there. At the time, she worked for the UN, the United Nations. While there, she met the colonel, they had a short affair, and I am the fruit of their romantic liaison. Rich was startled by this blunt and unexpected revelation. Since Andy had never mentioned anything, he boldly asked if Andy knew she was his daughter. This time he was in complete disbelief to learn that the colonel was unaware of the father-daughter relationship. Rich felt a bit sad for both Sabine and her mother and for Andy, who had been kept in the dark. The agent thanked her for trusting him enough to share this confidential information. Sabine remained quiet, and Rich started the car.

The agent brought himself back to the task and went over Sabine's assignment. "When I get down, off the roof, and land in the front of the building, I will call you on the comms unit. I want you to drive up the driveway of the mansion with your lights on, as far as the main building's front door." Rich watched Sabine's face for some reaction; there was none. "With this deliberate trespassing, someone will come out of that building to investigate this intrusion. When they do, I will be waiting, and I hope to be able to put the guy down using the chloroform; if this approach fails, you will have to shoot him." Rich studied Sabine's face following his demand for her to kill someone, and again there was no reaction. Please remember, if, at all possible, I need to get Pierre Paquet alive. To reach his office in the annex, I will need to back up, and I will depend on you to secure my move." Rich observed Sabine's composure. He was surprised once more; she remained calm and focused.

"Do not worry; I want him alive also."

Sabine's reaction to the situation left Rich perplexed. He had expected her to accept only a more passive role. Instead, without the least objection, she was ready to face risky conditions. He appreciated Sabine's sincere dedication to the operation and realized he had misjudged her capacity to encounter anything.

Without a word, Rich handed Sabine a comms unit, pulled his on, and made contact. "Can you hear me?"

"Loud and clear, we are ready. I have waited a long time for this.

CHAPTER 11

N PREPARATION FOR THE ATTACK, RICH APPLIED LAMP black below his eyes and on his face. He did not want any light to shine off his skin. After working his way through shrubs, he stopped to study the slow rotation of a camera attached to the corner of the building, timing the unit as it made a pass back and forth. There was no more time for planning. When the camera reached its return point, Rich ran like a deer across the yard, then fully erect, the agent pushed his back against the wall; he had made it in less than three seconds. The tough part was yet to come. He carefully watched the camera once again. Then, he stepped out at the right moment, threw the hook up over the top of the building, firmly pulled on the rope, and stepped back against the wall before the camera made its round. Just at the right time, he started his climb with only eight-plus seconds to complete the ascension. As his feet hit the wall, Rich moved upward. Just as the camera was to have him in view, he threw a rag over the lens, making the picture blurry to anyone watching.

Now on the roof, Rich pulled up the rope, formed a loop with it, and slid it over his shoulder. He would need it for the descent. To play it safe, he stepped softly near the peak of the slates. While stopping to catch his breath, the agent noticed the eastern sky giving place to a new day with rays of light timidly shining through the overcast. There was no time to waste; it would be daylight soon. From his mirador, he looked down for guards patrolling the premises; none was present. But crossing over to another part of the roof, he observed a man strolling beside the building. Rich just waited and watched as the guard slowly moved away. He contacted Sabine.

"I'm going to drop to the ground and approach the porch any minute."

"I am ready."

"Roger that." He thought, why in the hell am I saying that; I am retired from the Corps. "Let's stay silent unless a problem should arise." Rich watched and timed how long it was taking the guard to go around the building. The vigil started his second round. Rich took a deep breath, gripped the rope, and descended to the ground below. Then he pulled the line against the wall and hugged the corner of the building before touching terra firma. He felt and squeezed the small bottle of chloroform in his pocket. Rich had watched the man's movements and was not confident about holding him long enough to put him to sleep with the anesthetic. Instead, he took out the razor-sharp seal knife and held it ready.

A few seconds later, the guard stepped around the corner of the building. At that instance, Rich forcefully brought his hand over the man's mouth and nose and, with his right hand, brought the razor-sharp edge across his neck, from left to right. The blood squirted from the slashed arteries. There was no sound after lacerating the casualty's vocal cords. "Guard down," Rich said softly into his voice mike. He moved to the front of the building, a few feet from the main entrance door."

"Sabine, are you ready?"

"Been ready; give me the signal."

"Get out of the car. Have your gun ready. If I can't take the next bastard down, shoot him in his body mass at least three times. He will probably be wearing body armor, but with three shots, he won't be able to breathe for a few seconds. That will give me time. Go now."

As Sabine drove up into the grass-covered driveway, the front door of the house opened. Oblivious of the imminent danger, a man with an AR15 pointing toward stepped out. Sabine's fingers twitched. She was a bit nervous and scared too. By then, she had stepped out of the car. She could see that her bright headlights temporarily blinded the man who immediately shielded his eyes. Rich, with his knife in hand, leaped over the man who, now aware of imminent danger, made a run for it. At this time, there were three quick puff, puff, and puff sounds, much like that of a BB gun, as Sabine's silenced Glock 40 hit the man twice in the side and once in the back fell forward. Rich would not have to cut the guard's throat after all; the bullets had pierced through his heart. He had neglected to wear his bulletproof vest.

Sabine, with her gun ready, turned the headlights off immediately and waited for orders. Speaking softly into his mouthpiece, Rich said, "You are going to join me now. Stay a few feet behind. I will go to the right, so cover the left and stay low." Rich was now entering the building. The first thing he noticed in the large entryway was a long wrought iron coat rack holding several jackets, raincoats, and ceramic body armors. The first opening was to his left. Kneeling, he duck walked into a large chamber where lights were flashing in the very back. As he moved forward, he noticed the flickering was due to a TV that a man, slumped on an old wrinkled leather sofa, was watching. Sabine was still in the hall. Rich pointed for her to go left, and with his fingers, he indicated that he was entering the large room. Within seconds, without a sound, the agent was kneeling behind the couch, and Sabine was in place to protect him. Rich placed the barrel of his Sig against the man's head and said, "Stand up slowly, Paquet, and step forward with your hands up." He had recognized the leader of the pack, Pierre Paquet. The man stood up slowly, and fearless, shouted: "Allez vous faire foutre," (go get fucked.)

Alarmed by the noise, another man stepped into the room. Without hesitation, Sabine shot him in the right knee before he could draw a weapon. Rich addressed Paquet, "Stop your frog language; I know you speak English. We are going to have a little talk." With an expression of anger on his face, he yelled with defiance as he stood still. The agent calmly informed his captive,

"When I ask a question, be coherent and don't lie. Otherwise, my partner will shoot you in the knee."

"Fuck you, assholes; I have men coming in at any time."

"First question, what is the address of your CEO?"

"Go to hell, you bastards, you won't get a word out of me."

There was a puff sound, followed by a sharp yell as Pierre grabbed his left ankle and lost his balance, still ranting and shouting insults. "You guys are dead." After a pause, Rich presented the second question,

"Who is the main CEO of the CCC group in the United States?"

"Tom Stone of the New York Times."

That was a swift response, Rich thought. "Wrong answer." This false information was immediately followed by another puff sound, which resulted in the fall of Pierre. Now on the floor, the angry man was grabbing his right knee and screaming with pain. There had been only cursing and moaning coming out of him. Rich walked over to Sabine just a few feet away. "Paquet is not going to talk without some serious persuasion. Can you find me some light rope, if not, take out their shoestrings while I keep an eye on them."

CHAPTER 12

S ABINE WENT OUTSIDE TO LOOK FOR ROPES IN THE CAR. Finding none, she removed the shoestrings from the dead guard's high boots. Once back inside, Rich said, "Keep your gun on our friend, if he gives us trouble, you shoot him in the other foot." Pierre never said a word as Rich tied his arms behind his back, and his legs together. Wounded and tied up, the two guards looked pretty harmless. The agent turned to Sabine and said, "Keep an eye on them; I need to take a leak." After zipping up his pants, he emptied a small plastic wastepaper basket and filled it with water. Rich had seen the Central Intelligence Agency (CIA) use waterboarding on terrorists. This terrifying method to obtain information always worked, but no one was ever sure the answers resulting from the torture were correct. One could say anything, true or false, to stop the fear of drowning. As he walked back into the room, Rich addressed Sabine, "Keep watching our friends. I am taking Pierre in the bathroom. He needs a little head swim to loosen his tongue."

Pierre knew what was coming, he started screaming in French, then switched to English, yelling that it was against international law to waterboard. The agent replied,

"We are not sanctioned by any country that signed the law. Time to refresh you." Rich heard a puff coming from the other room. Sabine's action meant one less threat. Having disabled her captive, she hurriedly entered the large bathroom, and with a grin on her face, and an excited voice, she said, "Don't start without me. I have never witnessed waterboarding, and I have a feeling you are going to need help." Paquet was short, skinny, and wiry. The little man did not look like someone who was a weightlifting club member, but his strength was beyond belief. Even though he had been injured twice, and was restrained, he fought his captors vigorously to avoid the torture he was anticipating with fear. Rich sent Sabine back to the car to fetch a roll of duct tape, which she did after glancing at the other guard who was motionless on the floor. He was dead.

In the bathroom, along the wall, right below another wrought iron coat hanger, was a wooden bench painted in white. In preparation for the procedure, the agent folded a few towels that would be placed underneath Paquet's legs at one end of the bench to create an incline. A slope downward at the head was necessary to administer waterboarding. Rich lifted Pierre's chest onto the narrow board, grabbed the lower body, and dropped it on the plank, in line with the torso. To keep the martyr in place, Rich taped him tightly to the long seat and threw a wet washcloth over his face. Now unable to move, the punishment could start. Addressing Sabine, he said, "If you can stand it, I will ask you to pour the water over his face."

"Thank you for this important mission; I love to be useful."

Rich held in place the washcloth that covered Pierre's face as Sabine poured water over it. The captive tried to fight by jerking from left to right but fastened so tightly to the bench; he could not move. As expected, the liquid being poured over the face and nose immediately caused a gag reflex. It kept flowing, obstructing the nasal passages, and causing panic. To avoid drowning his captive, Rich ordered Sabine to give him a break; the torture was interrupted. "Give me the information I need, the address of the CEO here in France, and the name of the mystery man in the United States."

Water dribbled from Pierre's mouth as he was choking. "You, you will get nothing from me, fucker." As he uttered the last word, the washcloth was slapped back on his face, and Sabine grabbed the plastic wastebasket. "Give him some more."

As the water ran over the cloth, Sabine mumbled, "This is for all the women and girls you raped." Rich did not want to asphyxiate Paquet, not yet. Once more, the water was held back, and Pierre started breathing after spitting, coughing, and gagging. "What's the answer, prick?"

"F-f, fuck you," was the answer.

The plastic container was refilled, the soaked washcloth was spread over Pierre's face, and the procedure resumed. Soon, Pierre quit struggling; Rich gave Sabine the signal to stop. Worried, the agent turned Pierre's head to the side. The man started hacking, spitting, and finally, breathing. Following this last episode of waterboarding, Pierre appeared exhausted. Pale and with glaring eyes, he was now begging, "No more, no more, please. I will tell you what you want to know."

He gave them the name and address of the CEO in France. Then he revealed the identity of a chemical company CEO in Texas. He was ready to disclose anything to avoid further physical and mental pain. Still attached to the bench, he told the name of a United States senator and identified a member of the House of Representatives who worked for the CCC. Rich Had not expected to collect that much information. Drained from the traumatic ordeal, Pierre rolled and fell on the floor after the duct tape was removed. Rich coldly shot him in the head. The two partners sat down on the old wrinkled leather couch. "I got the info I wanted, and now there are less evil men in the world. We need to go."

Getting in the car, they had both noticed that the eastern facade of the building where several men were lying dead was fully illuminated by the bright sun. It was going to be a beautiful day, sunny and warm. Driving away, Sabine said, "I thank you for getting rid of these monsters. I have waited a long time to take my revenge on Pierre Paquet. Many women and girls owe you, Rich. Pierre was a dangerous man who is known to have raped several young women in the past."

The portion of the mission taking place in Paris was coming to an end. Sabine knew Rich would be on his way back to the States soon, but she had no idea when. She let him know she was available should he ever need help in the future.

Without warning, Sabine pulled off the road. She turned to face Rich. There was silence, and then she spoke, "When my mother was working for the UN, Pierre Paquet was employed in the security department of this international organization. One day, after hours, when most workers had left, he attempted to rape her in her office. Alarmed by the raucous this violation caused, one of the staff who was working late stepped in and stopped the assault. Due to the mentality that existed then regarding sexual crimes, Pierre got away with this unlawful act. Waterboarding this man was easy for me; I took revenge on behalf of my mother and others. Do you remember seeing a nice looking woman behind the counter at the cafe where we first met?" Rich nodded, and Sabine said, "That woman is my mom, she owns and runs this coffee shop." Rich gently put his left arm around Sabine's shoulder and told her to forget Paquet; the monster was dead.

He was relieved the guards had been eliminated, but most of all, he was grateful to have obtained valuable information. In a good mood, he made an offer to his dedicated partner,

"I would like to take you to dinner tonight. Can you make it?"

"Yes, I would like that, where do you want to meet me?"

"Not sure, do you know of a good place?"

"There is a wonderful restaurant on the Seine river. I will write the address down for you. Will seven p.m. be OK with you?"

"Seven is fine."

CHAPTER 13

HORNS WERE HONKING, AND PEOPLE WERE MOVING UP and down the streets as the bright rays of the sun engulfed Paris. Numerous thoughts were running through Rich's head as he drove into the parking garage at his hotel. He was dirty, hungry, and a bit troubled. He kept thinking about the surprising facts Sabine had shared with him, her mother's rape attempt, and earlier, Andy's paternity. He felt that sooner or later, the colonel should be told about this situation. He was sure that if the colonel had known Sabine was his daughter, she would not have been involved in such a dangerous mission. For the moment, the agent put his rambling thoughts aside and headed to his room. The shower he needed lasted three times longer than usual, the hot water spraying on his back, and his head was relaxing and brought his mind back to the present. It had been a tough day, but a good one. Rich turned the shower off at last and reached for the soft towel. While drying himself, he decided that he would call Ralph Wiggins, the FedEx pilot, to reserve a seat on a flight home. Next, Rich would send a coded message to the colonel to let him know what had transpired. He would also ask him where the unfinished mission would take him next. As he put his somewhat soiled pants and shirt back on, Rich realized his clothes were not adequate for that particular date in a nice restaurant.

He sat on the edge of his bed, picked up one of his burner phones, dialed the pilot, and after the fifth ring and no answer, sat the phone aside and headed to the hotel reception to find out where, in this neighborhood, one could buy decent clothes. As Rich took the red-carpeted stairs to the hotel entryway, he took out the card that Ralph had given him and redialed his number. On the third ring, the FedEx aircraft captain answered. "Good to hear from you. How was your stay in Paris?"

"I met with the company representatives as planned. I am exhausted, worn out. I decided to head back home early. Do you have any first-class seats available?"

After Ralph finished laughing, he said, "We have one first-class seat to DC at a discount at 12:30 a.m.

"I will take it. I presume I follow the same procedure as before."

"Roger that. This time, bring along a sandwich. I will have extra coffee for you."

"Thanks, cap. See you at eleven plus."

The desk manager was eager to assist Rich. He sent him to a store specializing in men's clothes that happened to be less than half a mile away. All the time Rich was walking, he mumbled, complaining how much he hated shopping for clothes. The agent took a deep breath and walked into Aux Hommes Bien Mis, a store specializing in men's quality garments. There he was approached by a salesman about his age who surprised him when he started speaking perfect English. Rich explained what he wanted: pants, shirt, and jacket, nothing eccentric or too conservative. Looking into a mirror, he approved of the salesperson's choice, gray trousers, a white shirt, and always in style, a tweed jacket. Also purchased were black socks and a pair of black leather loafers.

Early evening, Rich made contact with Colonel Coleman. He used code words before he informed Andy that all three men had been terminated. When the colonel asked if Sabine had performed to his satisfaction, Rich quickly responded, "Without her, the assignment would have been overly challenging." He closed the conversation by letting the colonel know he was heading to Texas and was expecting information concerning his next assignment after landing in Dallas.

The short drive to the restaurant seemed to take forever in the hectic traffic. Rich appreciated the instructions delivered by the GPS that Sabine had so kindly programmed. She knew that driving the streets of Paris was a nightmare.

CHAPTER 14

Paris, Seine River

SHADOWS BEGAN TO FORM ON THE BUILDINGS LINING the wide street parallel to the Seine River. He found a place to park on his fourth run past the meeting place, three blocks from his destination. The restaurant was located on a boat moored along the pier, adjacent to a quiet shady street lined with majestic plane trees. Along the river, children were walking hand in hand with their mothers. Seniors were slowly walking their dogs, and others were simply staring at the water from benches found under the dense canopy of the trees. The sun was casting even more shadows as Rich approached the floating restaurant Chez Rollo, an eatery specializing in dishes served in the French region of Normandy.

He knew that was the right address when he spotted the sign that read Bateaux Parisians Seine River Dinner Cruise. Stairs led down to the dining room. Rich looked up and down the street, then looked at his watch; it was six-forty three p.m. He hoped that Sabine would be early, for he felt exposed as he stood there with his hands on the railing. To kill time, he watched the passing Parisian women. Being busy most of the time, Rich never took a moment to notice how, in Paris, women had a different allure from the ones in his hometown. He could not quite explain that certain something that rendered them more attractive and more feminine. Maybe it was their attire's simplicity, the way their hair flowed naturally, or their slim figure that drew his attention. Perhaps it was also the way men, old and young, seem to admire them secretly.

Soon, a small and gentle hand tapped Rich's left arm, "Good evening, how about taking a lady to dinner?"

Rich was speechless; Sabine looked so different. For this particular date, she was wearing a knee-length slit gray pencil skirt that accentuated her petite waist and tastefully matched her leopard print blouse. A light beige trench coat was completing her looks. To add to her tasteful style, Sabine was wearing black pointed toe leather pumps.

It was several seconds before Rich gathered his thoughts, and after exchanging a few words, the two partners walked down the stairs, and onto the boat. Rich never understood what Sabine said to the waiter who was consulting a screen. Within a minute, they were led to a cozy and private table for two. Surrounded by glass, Rich stood in aw as he looked at the splendid view of the city of light and the river. He asked Sabine if Chez Rollo was an Italian restaurant. After all, the name suggested just that. Sabine explained that Rollo was the name of a Viking, a Northman, who, in the ninth century AD, became the first ruler of Normandy. Normandy is a province in northwestern France. The restaurant was known for its seafood and all sorts of delicacies cooked in heavy cream. All the time she was talking with animation, Rich stared into Sabine's green eyes. He was mesmerized and did not notice the waiter come up. Sabine ordered a bottle of Château du Bois de la Garde, a red wine. After they ordered mussels simmered in a shallot flavored white wine broth and poached sole served with a thickened butter-egg-and-cream sauce, they talked until their food arrived. The dinner was delicious, and Rich was savoring each mouthful.

It was getting late. After spending three hours eating and enjoying each other's company, it was time for Rich to get on the road, he had to return his rental car and be at the airport by eleven. Rich took a last sip of wine and said, "I think I have died and gone to heaven. Unfortunately, I have to be at the airport in one hour."

Sabine was taken aback. She had no idea Rich was returning to the States so soon. Most of all, she was vexed with him for not letting her know in advance of his plans to leave. Visibly disheartened, she chose not to say anything. Rich detected her disappointment, all he said was, "Sorry, you have my phone number, and I have yours. I know you want to come to the States to continue hunting members of the CCC there. I hope you will, for you are a better field operator than some I have worked with."

There was no verbal response, but her feelings could be read on her face. After paying the waiter, Rich and Sabine walked back up the stairs. He said, "I don't want to leave, but I must." His imminent departure did not bother her; the lack of courtesy did; she would have liked to be informed of his decision to leave that evening. She could not understand his behavior and found his attitude uncultured. With a bit of sarcasm, she gave him a lesson in civility.

"You must not have been around many women; if you had, you would know that they like to be treated kindly and with thoughtfulness. Your unexpected and sudden departure surprises me. I hope you have a safe trip." Feeling a bit sheepish for his lack of tact, Rich held Sabine's hands for a few seconds, said goodbye, and headed for his vehicle.

It was eleven p.m. when Rich turned in the rental car. He checked the time, then hurried to meet Captain Ralph, the pilot of the FedEx plane. Disturbed by the disastrous ending of the evening, Rich had forgotten to buy a sandwich or even an apple for the long flight back to Washington DC. Four hours into the flight, Ralph brought out coffee. "We will be landing in just under four hours. Clearing through customs back home is not as easy as in Paris. Have your passport ready, and make sure the home address you give the agent is correct." Ralph blinked; he knew Rich was using a different passport while operating in Paris.

"In a few more years, it will be like Nazi Germany the way the government is controlling its citizens," Rich said as he smiled back dryly. "All the cameras and screenings became common after the 9/11 fiasco. Most likely, members of the CCC and our government agreed on letting 9/11 happen. I hope that someday the investigation reports will be released, and maybe then, someone will speak out." Rich took a deep breath and continued. "The people in America are sheeple. They believe anything they hear. I feel it is too late to get our old times back."

"You must remember the senator who resigned because of intelligence personnel telling the investigation committee what to write." There were several seconds of silence, then Ralph continued. "By the way, what is the CCC?"

"The CCC stands for Council Corporate Control and is an organization that controls the White House. The group membership consists mostly of rich people and CEOs." Rich could see that Ralph was in disbelief, stunned even.

Rich finished his coffee, closed his eyes, and slept until the plane shuttered as the wheels lowered. A crunching noise followed when the landing gear locked in place. Just over a minute passed before the aircraft bounced on impact. The high pitched whining of the turbines brought Rich's hands to his ears while the plane decelerated. Once the big cargo plane came to a sudden stop, the agent unbuckled and waited for Ralph. He wanted to be out of the airport as fast as he could. While walking to the FedEx office, Rich asked Ralph if, by chance, he knew anyone who could give him a ride to Texas?"

Ralph studied Rich for a few seconds and said, "I know of only one person; another FedEx pilot. When do you want to go?"

"Tonight or tomorrow morning. I will pay for the ride."

"I know that my friend Jonathan Wright flies out at seven a.m. tomorrow morning. What name will you be using if I call him?"

"The same one I used with you."

Ralph took out his cell phone, walked away from Rich, about twenty feet, and dialed his friend. Five minutes had passed before Ralph walked came and said, "Be here, at this office, before six a.m. You will put on a FedEx employee's suit again." Ralph laughed and put his cell phone back in his pocket. Rich handed the pilot a few hundred dollars bills and thanked him for his service. Ralph tried to give the money back, but Rich was already on his way to rent a vehicle. At the Dollar Rental office, the agent found what he wanted, a dark-colored Toyota Camry. Once again, out of habit, Rich looked the vehicle over carefully before opening the door to place his two packs on the back seat. As the engine warmed up, Rich slid over his shoulder his fast draw holster holding the gun of one of the dead men he had eliminated in Paris.

Before leaving, he set the rearview mirrors to watch if an unwelcome someone might be tailing him. After driving for an hour, he pulled into a small mall and parked in front of DC Secure Mailbox rentals, where he and the colonel shared a mailbox. This UPS business was just two miles from his condo. Rich showed the young man at the desk the proper ID that would allow him access to the box inside of which he kept funds and supplies. He knew he had a slim chance to find a folder or package concerning his next job. He retrieved two new passports, some cash, a Glock Forty, several filled mags, and a silencer.

The colonel had dropped a large brown envelope. Rich was a little anxious as he picked it up. He looked around the room for a seat, found a chair with no padding or arms, and opened the packet. The agent carefully slid out the contents to which several photos were attached. Putting the pictures aside, Rich began to read. "Here is a list of people in high places who, in the past, might have worked with the group." Rich was shocked to discover that former presidents and others holding high positions were listed. Some were Republican and some Democrat. Rich picked up the papers dealing with his next assignment. After reading the first two pages, he looked at the list of players he was to terminate in Texas, and decided to return the documents to their envelope. Rich would go over everything thoroughly in the more relaxing surroundings of his condo. After stretching his legs, he returned to his vehicle, started the engine, and headed toward his residence. Once there, the agent was pleased to find the two traps left behind, a hair, and a small piece of paper, still in place between the side of his front door and the door jamb. After showering and going through his mail, Rich paid bills, packed some clothes, gathered funds, added two sets of night goggles, and new armory to his pack.

That evening Rich fell asleep within minutes. Eight hours later, the orange glow of the sun could be seen toward the east as he drove down his street, pulled right, and headed for the airport.

After turning in his Camry, Rich looked at his watch; it was only five-twenty a.m. Inside the terminal, he found a store selling sandwiches, bottles of water, and fruits. No way would he starve himself on this flight. Now at the FedEx office, loaded with his two packed backpacks, the agent looked around for a flight captain with a name tag identifying Johnathan Wright. Seeing none, Rich sat down after telling the clerk he was waiting for someone. At precisely six a.m. Captain Johnathan Wright, dressed in a pair of blue trousers, a white shirt, a tie, and a name tag bearing his name, arrived. He walked into the room, immediately spotted Rich, whom he approached with his hand out.

After the two men chatted for a while, Johnathan had Rich follow him into the pilot's small rest area and handed him a pair of large brown coveralls. "Slip these over your clothes, and follow me." As they walked across the tarmac toward the plane, the sun rose on the horizon, and soon it would drench the city. Acting like this was a routine operation, the two men walked out and got on the FedEx plane, scheduled to leave for Dallas, Texas.

CHAPTER 15
Texas

DURING THE FLIGHT, JOHN BROUGHT OUT COFFEE and spent a few minutes with his guest. He was intrigued by the CCC and needed information to satisfy his curiosity. Over Coffee, Rich told him as much as he could, never once did the pilot ask Rich the reason for his travel or his connection with Ralph.

When John announced they would be landing within an hour, Rich handed the captain a roll of hundred dollar bills. At first, John said he did not have to do this as he was doing Ralph a favor. Rich responded, "I might need another flight home someday." The agent continued to make eye contact, and said, "I don't know what Ralph told you, but I want you to know that I am not dealing in any illegal activities. I work for a clandestine organization, and have to stay off the grid." John placed the money in his pocket and said, "Here is my phone number if you ever need a ride." He handed Rich a business card before returning to the cockpit.

Rich emptied his bottled water, cinched up his seat belt, and closed his eyes. It seemed like only minutes had passed when he heard the landing gear drop; within minutes, the plane bounced several times, then there was a high pitch squeal as the turbines reversed. The agent was a bit anxious to get off the plane. He followed John inside the FedEx office, removed his coveralls, and headed for the car rental in his Levis and pullover shirt. His leather jacket dissimulated his Glock 40. The gun he had inherited from one of his victims in France was now in his backpack.

After registering for a black Ford SUV, Rich headed into the terminal to buy a Texas road map and several geographical maps of Texas. One particular topographical map included the layout of a ranch owned by a chemical company CEO, a member of the CCC.

Before Rich left the Dallas airport, he studied again the pictures of individuals he had been carrying in his backpack. He wrote the name of the person on the back of each photograph. Then he examined the names of the Texan chemical enterprises mentioned. It seemed that almost all of the leading companies were on the list. Rich read a short brief about each one. He wondered why he was expected to go to Kermit, Texas, a town of 6500 plus inhabitants located in the north-west of the state when the companies in question had their head offices in Houston and Galveston, at the extreme opposite of Kermit. He read on and found the reason for the side trip to that small town.

A wealthy oil tycoon owned a seven hundred twenty-five thousand-acre ranch NW of Kermit, Texas, and over two hundred thousand acres across the New Mexico border, an arid area. For a fee, the ranch offered a five-day exotic game hunt where the targets consisted of imported wild animals such as Nubian Ibexes, Mouflon sheep, Blackbucks. Rich was instructed that the ranch owner, a CCC man, was scheduled to welcome and entertain a group of CCC members at his ranch.

Rich turned the page and read the name of the man in charge of security, Captain Spencer, special forces, retired. The dossier pointed out Spencer's experience and his qualifications, details that alarmed the agent. This Spencer individual was well trained as a killer. Under his command, ten other guards, including green berets, special Army forces, and even one former Delta member, were also responsible for protecting the ranch. A note at the bottom of the list read that a total of twenty men worked on the security detail. Rich turned to his orders. He was expected to terminate Captain Spencer, CEOs Wilderson, and Ringgold, and if possible, as many of the top five men serving under Spencer. The message encouraged Rich to do what he could while being extremely careful. A piece of news read that the responsible authors of a leak in the White House were now down to two names.

Before leaving Dallas, Rich bought and filled four five-gallon jeep gas cans. With a disguise in place, he purchased dried food and a good emergency medical kit. He then bribed a medical supply employee for lidocaine and antibiotics. After changing clothes, the agent put on his colored eye lenses before driving to different gun shops in Dallas's offbeat areas. Next, he bought two good Remington 700s with scopes and chambered for 308 loads. Rich ended up spending over ten thousand dollars for the guns and the particular loaded 308 ammo he wanted. But the expense was worth it as there was no record of purchase, checks, or identity involved.

During a late lunch, he googled the ranch under Safaris and big-game hunt in Texas. He realized he would need a powered hand glider to check out the arroyos, those deep-sided gullies, and surrounding areas. After looking over the ranch contour map, he realized he could not do the work alone. There was only one person who could fit the job, Sabine. He finished his steak, took a sip of beer, and pulled a burner phone from his pack. The agent looked at his watch. With the time difference in Paris, it was almost midnight there. From memory, he pushed in the digits for Sabine's phone. On the eighth ring, without any greeting, a soft sleepy voice said, "You take a lady to dinner, leave her hanging, and suddenly disappear. And now you have the nerve to startle her in the middle of the night. Do you know it is midnight here?" There was a long pause, then she added, "What is the purpose of this late call?"

Rich realized she was still bitter over his hurried departure. He decided not to go over that again; he simply said, "I need your help."

Sabine started showing some interest right away, and her sarcastic approach disappeared, "OK, what do you need me to do?"

"I have five days to recon a mega ranch here, in Texas, and try to eliminate several CCC members and their watchdogs. I warn you, it is a dangerous project, and it could be a one-way trip. I thought about you; I know how much you despise the group, and I also know you are a skilled shooter."

"No matter what the difficulty of the job, hunting those scums will give me great pleasure,-------- count me in. When should I leave?"

"I need time to recon the area and drop in some supplies. I will book your flight on British Airways straight to Dallas on Thursday, three days from now. Will that be OK?"

Sabine knew it was, but she wanted Rich to worry a little, so she took her time to answer. "That will be fine with me. At what time will my plane leave Paris?"

"I do not have the details right now, but there is a flight that lands in Dallas at 3:20 p.m. Bring what you think you will need, you can get the rest here. You will be getting your plane tickets and schedule within an hour."

"I hope you will give me a chance to practice with a rifle. I have not used one in some time."

"Yes, of course. I will pick you up at the airport outside the main gate. Just look for me, remain cautious. After you spot me, just follow ten or twenty paces behind. We will work our way to a car rental. Damn it, Sabine, I got ahead of myself. I will be glad to see you again. Forgive me, but I have to go."

Rich took care of Sabine's first-class reservation and sent her a message reinforcing the details concerning their meeting at the Dallas airport, time, and place. That done, the agent felt relieved that his partner had accepted the deal. To execute his plans, he needed a glider. He found a powered hand glider rental, sales, and instruction shop, located on a small ranch outside of Dallas. After taking lessons for three hours, he asked the owner if he had a glider with more power. Without hesitation, the owner said he had this hand glider that could easily take off with over seven hundred pounds of cargo. Rich walked with the owner to look at the larger unit. As Rich checked it out, he noticed there were oversized low-pressure tires for sand and a small storage area. Satisfied, the agent put a downpayment on the beefed-up powered hand glider tandem and told his instructor he would come by the following morning for more practice. If feeling secure in operating the unit, he would take it that day.

Later Rich drove out highway 20 down to Kermit, some four hundred miles, then took road 285 north to Orla, not far from the New Mexico border. It did not take long for Rich to find the Texas Wild Life Hunting Ranch with its doorless massive cast-iron gate with, at the top, a decorative sign that read African Safari Hunting. On both sides were the six feet tall silhouetted images of a Nubian ibex in semi-profile. After driving by the front entrance, he stopped on the edge of the road, took out his binoculars, and scoped the area. Parked nearby were a helicopter and a small plane bearing an emblem representing an Axis deer's head with its large recurved horns. Rich planned to make both units inoperable before the attack on the ranch.

After finishing scoping the area, the agent passed the front entrance once more. He remained as invisible as possible; this semi-arid region offered no place to hide. Trying not to look suspicious, he drove around the fenced-in game ranch, took pictures, and recorded notes. The openness, the size of the site, everything indicated that even with proper preparation, the task to take out the members of the CCC would be hellish. As he drove to the northeast, Rich found a dirt road going into the western side of the game ranch. There he noticed that the bed of a dry creek at the bottom of an arroyo led up toward the ranch area. That was an important finding.

The next thing to locate on his journey was the four other roads indicated on the map, and finding where they opened on to, should an emergency escape from the area be needed.

It was close to 2:00 a.m. when Rich left Kermit and, after driving for hours, reached the outskirts of Dallas, tired and covered with sand and sweat.

CHAPTER 16

THE ORANGE HUE OF THE RISING SUN APPEARED ON the horizon as it began its upward journey in the clear sky. The humidity was palpable even though it was early morning. The heat and the dampness would not keep Rich from his daily routine; he did one hundred pushups on the lawn of the deserted motel, then went for a five-mile run as the sun climbed into the blue sky. Soaking wet with sweat, a shower was needed. After toweling off, he put on jeans, a dark brown pullover, and headed for a small restaurant down the street.

It was eight a.m. when Rich reported for his lesson at the small airport. He was ready for instructions to become competent to pilot the powered hand glider, for he wanted to take it with him after lunch.

For several hours Rich performed take-off and landing over and over. Finally, the instructor declared him ready to handle the small aircraft. It was after one p.m. when Rich signed the necessary papers to complete the purchase. Then, inquiring about renting a trailer, the salesman mentioned having a used one for sale. After completing the second set of paperwork for this second acquisition, the two men loaded and secured the aircraft onto the trailer.

Rich's next task was to find two stolen license plates and a lightweight dirt bike. He found a Magician Dual Sports bike undoubtedly capable of carrying two people. Before taking the motorcycle, he had the shop strip the bike to keep its weight down before loading it on the trailer. He headed out of town to practice riding the bike on the vast flatlands and rolling hills outside the city. It did not take him long to handle the unit up and down small hills and over ruts. That done, Rich drove back into town to gather the remaining items needed for the assault and track down two license plates. At a large mall, he furtively picked up the necessary items. It was eight p.m. when Rich finally ate dinner, followed by a short walk and a shower before hitting the sack.

Just after three a.m. the following morning, Rich headed back to Kermit and Orla. Once he found the dirt road discovered the day before, he drove toward the dry creek bed. After going as far as he could, on flat terrain, he unloaded the powered hand glider. As the sun was pushing upward toward nine a.m., Rich pushed the throttle forward. Assisted by the thermals coming off the desert, the hand glider soon was airborne. The agent glided at low altitude while staying parallel to the massive 725,000 plus acre ranch. Rich saw numerous wild game from the air and spotted solar panels used to pump water in this arid land where only a few springs existed. As he flew, he kept in mind that he had to put together a plan for an emergency escape should the project to eliminate the CCC members fail. From the air, Rich noticed a deep arroyo with a dry sand base, long and wide enough for him to glide in and park on the sandy bottom. After landing smoothly,

Rich covered the glider with a camouflage net in the dead-end arroyo. He took out his field glasses and a bottle of water, then started the long walk toward the game ranch. Suddenly the silence of the semi-desert area broke into a deafening cacophony as hundreds of birds flew from thorny bushes and water-deprived poplars. That unexpected racket surprised and even scared Rich. He continued down the arroyo and was startled once more when several antelopes and a few gazelles came out with speed and agility from behind a stand of poplars. Speechless and motionless, Rich just stared at these shy small horned creatures which were destined to be hunted for a hefty fee by vain individuals. As he turned right into a branch of the creek bed, all of a sudden, rolling in the mud, were several warthogs. Those African wild pigs with their large heads and impressive curved tusks caused Rich to move at a safe distance up the slope of the ravine.

An hour had passed when he approached the ranch headquarters. From far away, flat on his belly, Rich studied the guards' rotation and the frequency at which patrols conducted by SUVs and motorcycles were scheduled.

Over eight hours had passed before he had a good idea regarding the surveillance routine of the ranch. Using his compass, he returned to check on his glider and loaded two gasoline can on it before returning to his SUV on the motorcycle. The fuel would be available to get himself and Sabine back to the SUV after the assassination. Rich still wanted to drive up into New Mexico to see how far the ranch extended and keep an eye on possible escape routes.

The next morning the temperature was more temperate. The agent returned to the ravine to fly his glider. Thermals that had helped get the powered aircraft airborne the day before were not present at this time. After almost six hundred feet, the powered hand glider slowly lifted off the ground. Coming back, the landing in the wash was a little rough. After pulling to a stop, he examined his unit; there was no damage. Before leaving, the agent planted booby traps in the sand every three hundred feet in the opposite way he and Sabine would be escaping. Rich set these charges off to kill but also to create dust when exploding. He lifted off once more with the glider and returned to his SUV. Rich drove back to Dallas using a different route, always keeping an eye out for someone tailing him. The drive back to the city seemed twice as long as before. Rich was covered with sweat and dirt, and could not wait for a good shower and a meal.

In Paris, Sabine had communicated with Rich at intervals and was now ready for her journey to Texas.

On his way to Dallas Ft. Worth airport, the agent stopped just outside of city limits at a cowboy bar and loan shop. Two days before, he had stopped there to buy some rifles and had ordered two sets of AR550 body armor and ten timers. Once again, Rich made sure he had on his disguise. After paying the balance for this off the books deal, Rich hid the supplies in his SUV. It was essential to have the timers as he had already placed explosives in strategic spots. Following the project's execution, Rich was planning to blow up the motorbike, the trailer, and the SUV. As he was leaving the illicit store, he mumbled out loud. "One thing about Texas, if you have the money, you can buy almost anything."

Rich was now on his way to the airport.

CHAPTER 17

I T WAS 2:30 P.M. WHEN RICH DROVE THROUGH THE GATE at Dallas Ft. Worth airport. Inside the airport, the agent consulted the first flight information display. The inbound British Airways flight was on schedule. Having time to kill, Rich headed to the closest cafe to get a beer and relax. Meeting Sabine was a bit stressful for Rich. His inexcusable behavior in Paris had caused some misunderstanding between the partners, which he hoped would not affect the outcome of the project he had spent days preparing.

He moved in and out around people before heading for the customs area outside the main building. Rich became impatient and began pacing, being careful to stay away from cameras. He was a bit apprehensive, but also happy to welcome Sabine to Texas. He liked to converse with her. She was very friendly, witty, and could be funny at times.

Rich stood in the background for thirty minutes to avoid the traffic of passengers moving through the luggage claim and customs. Finally, he spotted his partner. Even after a long flight that had not been direct, and included a two-hour layover in Atlanta, Sabine was radiant.

From his spot, he was observing her with attention, discovering that physically, she was cute, attractive, and offered many physical attributes. In Paris, he had valued her intelligence and common sense but had been too business-like and too focused on the job to appreciate her other qualities. He came out of his dreamlike state when he saw her approaching him fast.

Sabine had made sure to wear her stretch black two-button blazer with matching ankle pants that exposed her sexy shoes and enhanced her lean body. This tasteful ensemble included a plain gray tee shirt. She moved forward, carrying a leather tote bag in one hand, and pulling a small carry on suitcase with the other. She stood out in this crowd, and men discreetly gazed at her as she moved up the hallway toward the exit. As Sabine left the building, she saw her partner, and this first visual contact brought a big smile on her face.

Sabine was beaming as she approached. This display of good spirits reassured the agent. She grabbed his hand and held it as they greeted each other in a friendly manner. Rich thanked her repetitiously for accepting to help him with his project.

He pulled the carry on suitcase behind him as he and Sabine walked toward the parking area. His partner was more open and expressive than Rich; she was reserved but not shy. She made her partner a happy man when she said, "I am so glad to see you again, and I hope you have a lot planned for us so we can spend some memorable times together." He was not sure what she meant, but it sounded promising.

"We will be busy tomorrow. If you are not too tired, I would like to take you for a good Texas meal while we are in Dallas. Tomorrow we will leave on a long ride to Kermit, where I will give you your first glider flight and an introduction to the ranch where the CCC members will have a get-together. So what about dinner?"

"Flying first class was beneficial, I slept on the way over, so I am ready to rustle a steer or two." They were now on the way to the hotel. "I rented you a room next to mine at the Residence Inn by Marriott." He noticed right away that she had let her hair down. Laughing, he stared at her and said, "You are so petite and feminine, what are you doing with me hunting down bad guys?"

"You know how much I despise the CCC, I hate those people as much as you do, maybe even more."

During the ten-plus mile ride, Rich explained to Sabine how he had prepared for the slaughter that would take place very soon.

It was almost 7:00 p.m. when Rich heard a knock on his hotel room door. Sabine entered. She had not changed for the evening, was still wearing her skinny jeans and her gray tee-shirt, and had brought along her trench coat. Her hair was twisted into a bun to add an inch or two to her petite build. It had been a very long day for her, and the time change between Paris and Dallas had extended it by seven hours.

The couple left for the famous Flora Street Cafe, a warm, casual, and semi elegant restaurant. Rich wanted his partner to enjoy a real barbecue feast, the way it is prepared in Texas. He explained how mesquite wood most often was used for grilling the marinated meat, brisket, pork ribs, or sausages. They started the evening with a frozen margarita, accompanied by an assortment of mini tacos, tiny tostadas, and miniature enchiladas. The wine list included imported wines and, to the surprise of the partners, several Texan wines. Out of curiosity, Rich ordered a Texan wine, a Merlot, from the Llano Estacado winery. Neither of them knew that Texas grew grapes and exported part of its wine production. Their friendly waiter explained that with flat terrain covering much of the Panhandle, the Texas High Plains experienced long, hot, dry summers with cool evenings. The region's unique soil had an advantage; it drained well and kept the vineyards free of the louse that had plagued Californian and French winemakers for centuries. With the help of their waiter's suggestion, they ordered several cuts of meat and typical side dishes made of okra and beans.

In the meantime, they savored their drinks and the Mexican samplers. Both Rich and Sabine let the outside world drift away and enjoyed each other's company. The conversation was warm and animated.

Just after nine p.m., even though Sabine never complained about fatigue, Rich noticed that her eyes looked tired. He knew that she had been up since the early morning of the day before. Rich gently slapped her hand and said, "I think we better go, dear, we have to get up no later than 4:00 a.m.

Sabine thanked him for the meal, which she found to be so different from what she was accustomed to, and wished him a good night. Upon their return to the hotel, he handed her a pair of size small military fatigues. She was to put them on in the morning. Although exhausted, she found the energy to shower, finally went to bed and fell asleep in minutes. Once in his room, Rich's head had no more than hit the pillow; he fell asleep.

It was ten minutes to 4:00 a.m. when Rich phoned Sabine to wake her up. She yawned twice before he was able to get her attention. Rich reminded her they had to be on the road, and soon. "I am bringing you a cup of coffee." After hanging up, Rich filled a cup with black coffee and went to Sabine's room next door. He was surprised when she opened the door; his partner had the military fatigues on. "I will pick you up in ten minutes. We have a long drive ahead of us."

Posing in front of the large mirror in her room, dressed in her new military uniform, Sabine jokingly said, "Oui monsieur, commandant."

CHAPTER 18

I T WAS DARK WHEN THE COUPLE LEFT DALLAS. AS THEY drove along, Sabine was amazed by the vastness of the prairie. They continued to chat as they drove toward Abilene. In that city, Rich used a different driver's license to rent a second vehicle. Sabine would drive the new car. Just before leaving the rental agency, he handed her a phone with a pair of earplugs connected. "At any time, if you think you are too far back or think you have lost me, call. Just hit the speed dial, I will have a phone with the earplugs also."

He warned his partner that the trip was a long one. He gave Sabine a friendly tap on the shoulder before pulling out of the parking lot with his SUV and trailer. The hours dragged as they drove down highway 20, never exceeding the speed limit. When they reached the town of Pecos, they stopped in the parking lot of a small cafe. Rich got out of the car and walked over to Sabine's vehicle. "We better eat breakfast here." Before entering the cafe, Rich put on his disguise and had Sabine wear her wig and sunglasses. They ordered pancakes, eggs, and drank what seemed to amount to a gallon of coffee. Just before leaving, Rich ordered four ham and cheese sandwiches to go. The two units drove out onto the highway. Within a few miles, Rich made a sudden turn toward the small town of Orla and contacted Sabine on the short wave to tell her to stay close as they approached the place where they would leave her vehicle. Rich pulled off on a dirt road and soon parked. They would continue the journey with his SUV.

Sabine got in Rich's car. While she waited, Rich drove Sabine's vehicle into some brush and trees and covered it with camouflage netting. When he got back into the SUV, he announced, "We still have a long way to go, and it's going to be a rough ride as we get closer to the ranch. Strap in tight." The drive was dusty, and the SUV bounced as they hit the ruts. At times it felt like the trailer was coming loose. Soon, Rich drove down a deep arroyo and shut the SUV's engine off. "As promised, I am going to take you for a ride in my glider." She reminded him once more of her need to practice shooting, "Do you have the guns with you?"

"They're hidden under the seat. What kind of rifle and automatic pistols have you used?"

"I was trained in the use of a German FN FAL rifle and used the AK47 several times. The only handguns that I am proficient in are the Luger and the German police guns. I did use your Glock, as you know." Then she smiled and jokingly poked Rich in the side.

"What I want you to practice using is a Glock 40. It packs quite a punch. The nozzle tends to rise when you fire it. But let me tell you, if you hit anyone with it, they are going down."

Ten minutes later, Rich was sliding the powered motor glider from the trailer and down on the prairie grass and sandy soil. While preparing the aircraft, he reviewed details, answered questions, and emphasized the importance of following directions while flying, such as how and when to lean with the glider. To the east, Rich could see the slight twirl of dirt and sand in the small tornado-like thermals coming off the prairie, those warm current of air that would help with the take-off.

Rich had Sabine sit on the front seat. As he leaned forward to buckle her, he brushed her hair and could feel the warmth her luscious body gave off. He had never been so physically close to her. "We will go along the sand until the sail behind us picks up enough air to gain height. Just don't panic as you don't have something to lean against like on a plane."

"I am not worried. I trust you."

Rich had made five take-offs and landings before flying about three hundred feet above the dirt. Then he made several steep turns to get Sabine adjusted to the powered glider. They flew out onto the desert for several minutes before returning to the arroyo. Once back on land, Sabine said, "That was an exciting ride. Now I should be practicing shooting the Glock 40."

After returning the glider on the trailer, Rich took out two rifles, two handguns, plenty of ammo, and two silencers. It was time to sight in the Remingtons for long-range sniper use. Previously Rich had taken time to set up markers at 200, 500, 600, and 700 yards out.

Both Sabine and Rich had shot low on their targets initially, but after a dozen or more shots, they hit the mark. They worked with their scope until they became competent. "Why the silencer if we are out in the badlands?" Sabine stared at him, then blinked. She knew exactly why.

Rich handed her her lunch and a pair of surplus military-grade binoculars. After a one hour recess, Rich had Sabine put on a bulletproof vest and place her sidearm under her left shoulder. Then he handed her the rifle she would be using later. Instinctively, she made sure the silencer was in her pocket. She sat down on the front seat of the powered glider. Her partner climbed at the control and placed a weapon across his lap. He buckled in and kept his binoculars hanging against his chest.

The small engine howled as the tires picked up speed in the sandy dirt of the arroyo. At last, the wheels became free, they bounced and skimmed along the top of a small bush. As it approached a mound of dirt, the glider started to lift some. All of a sudden, a thermal filled the sail, and the small aircraft gained elevation. Sabine turned around to face Rich, her tan army hat was almost pulled down over her eyes, and there were beads of sweat creeping down the sides of her flushed cheeks. She said something that he did not hear. He pointed at the walkie talkie in her jacket and at his ear. Sabine turned on her unit and placed an earbud in her ear. As they continued getting closer to the single-story ranch houses, Rich was careful to keep the sail just above the top of the arroyo. He did not want to take any chance of being exposed to guards on patrol. Jokingly she declared, "You sure know how to give a person a thrill. After the mission is over, I refuse more adrenaline rushes. I may end up developing PTSD."

Rich brought the rudder stick back to bring the vehicle up. In his ear, he heard Sabine say, "Oh my, those are African animals."

"As I told you earlier, most of them were imported from Africa. Now the rancher breeds them. When they reach adulthood, rich hunters kill them with bow and arrows."

There was silence when Rich tilted the glider right, taking them even further to the east of the property so the sun's bright rays would be behind them. Rich said, "We will make another turn soon. Get your field glasses and look up ahead." There was a passel of African boars, probably twelve of them.

"You will have a chance to see more of the living targets later. Right now, we are going to land. Hang on." Deep in the arroyo, Rich pulled the throttle back, and the glider began to descend. Soon there was a bounce as the tires made contact with the sand, the vehicle slowed and stopped.

Rich made sure Sabine's bulletproof vest was on tight and secure, and with a rifle in hand, they walked to the ridge of the arroyo. For the next two hours, the two hitmen laid in the grass and timed the patrols surveilling the ranch. After returning to the bottom of the arroyo, Rich pulled out his notes about the patrol routine he had recorded a few days past and compared them with his recent observations. The timing was identical.

Rich took a small thermos out of his backpack. The two partners walked until they found some shade under some poplars. Sitting down under the trees, they shared some coffee. After this short recess, Sabine stood guard while Rich fueled the powered glider and the motorcycle. It was getting warm; they decided to remain in their safe and cool sanctuary to rest and wait until sunset.

Time passed slowly, giving Rich a chance to go over his plans several more times. To kill time, they ate their second ham and cheese sandwich and cleaned their rifles and handguns. As the sun was moving west, they changed their position several times. Rich assured himself Sabine had stored her rifle and handgun mags in her fatigues. He then checked to make sure her walkie talkie was secure, and the earbud was attached. He strapped on a razor-sharp knife to the outside of her right leg, smiled, and said, "The knife is just in case one of the hunters get up close and want to kiss you." Then he buckled on her ceramic bulletproof vest.

Sabine said, "I hope I don't have to run anywhere fast; this vest weighs a ton."

"We need all that equipment, and we will have to run only a short distance back to the dirt bike. The CCC is going to have an army similar to mad bees after us. They are already after me, but they have no idea we are working together. Keep your hair inside your cap and sunglasses on, and make damn sure you wear gloves. Oh, before I forget, place this lamp black under your eyes." Rich handed Sabine the small plastic container. "We don't want any glare from the sun." When Sabine finished with the lampblack, Rich applied some below his eyes and on his cheeks. After screwing the lid back on, he placed the small container in the pocket on his leg from which he took out Clorox wipes he handed to Sabine. "If you have to leave a gun behind, wipe it down with this as I do not want anyone to get your DNA." Rich continued to talk as he picked up the apple cores and sandwich wrappers, and put all the garbage in his backpack. The agent set the timing device in a pocket on his chest. He put several mags on his belt and made sure his extra, extra-large bulletproof vest was secure. Little did Sabine know that on their way out, with her riding on the back of the dirt bike, he would put his bulletproof vest over hers.

Rich checked Sabine once more, then his gear, and said, "Almost time to go, partner. Make sure you follow orders, and if I go down, take the dirt bike and head back to the arroyo where the SUV is, it should take less than half an hour. Rich then stepped close to Sabine, wrapped one arm around her shoulders, and pulled her against him. He worried about the danger that was to come. After a long firm squeeze, he gave her a quick peck on the cheek. This friendly, and maybe romantic behavior was uncommon coming from Rich and gave Sabine the impression the mission was not sure to end according to plans. This sudden demonstration of affection almost gave Sabine a sense of desperation. She started laughing and said, "Should death be in the cards, maybe we should cuddle before we go." Rich looked into Sabine's eyes and said, "I think you are interpreting the fondness I feel toward you right now as my way to reassure you before uncontrollable danger. Relax, I am confident we are going to be fine. Every detail of this project has been rehearsed to perfection; we are ready. We have only this one chance to catch the bad guys assembled in one place. We will be the victors." Sabine apologized for giving the impression she doubted her partner. Rich said, "I am not expressive, hugging you was just to let you know that I like you."

The couple, now holding hands, remained sitting on the sandy loam in complete silence. When it was time, Rich started walking toward the dirt bike.

CHAPTER 19

RICH PULLED THE DIRT BIKE FROM UNDERNEATH THE poplar trees. He started the engine and invited Sabine to take her place behind him. "It will be a tight fit, so I will pull my pack around to fit over my chest. Make sure you hold on tight, especially when the path becomes a little steep as we come up out of the arroyo."

"You don't have to worry. If I fall off, you are going with me." Rich laughed, then looked west toward the horizon. They had only about half an hour to reach their destination. He told Sabine that anyone shooting at them would have to be looking into the sun.

Because the soil was so dry, Rich drove slowly through the arroyo to prevent blinding dust clouds from rising. He stopped at intervals to place an electronic device in each explosive he had planted here and there a few days earlier. After the last one was set, Rich drove up a steep hill that opened onto the prairie with one foot on the ground to steady the bike. Now on flat ground, he asked Sabine for her field glasses to scrutinized in the ranch's direction to detect any patrolling activity and any unwanted presence in front and behind them. No sign of surveillance was detected. "We need to take the bike a mile closer to the ranch house where you see that stand of thick brush in front of us."

"This is where we are going to get off the bike and stay low. We will move another three to four hundred yards toward the ranch house where there is a deep gully, and this is where you will remain to provide cover for me. After I leave you, I will have to go another couple of hundred yards to the southeast to get a clear shot of the patio where the fiesta organized by the ranch owner in honor of several important members of the CCC will be taking place."

It took another five minutes for the two snipers to reach the gully where Sabine would serve as a spotter for Rich and provide cover fire after he retreats to that position. Once hidden in the ravine, they both stretched their tired muscles from having to bend over so long. Rich prepared her long gun and set her scope for the distance. Sabine handed him her silencer, and he screwed it on tight. Rich made sure she had two mags laid out for immediate use, and said, "If you use or don't use them, you must pick them up and put them back in your pack. Don't leave anything behind that can tie this operation to us." After going over the plan one more time, Rich took off his pack, took his long gun, and chambered a round. Then he reached into his pocket and replaced the bullet he had used from the mag and screwed on his silencer. "Now remember, if you change mags, be sure and place the empty one in your pack. Any evidence left behind can jeopardize our mission. It's important."

Without saying a word, he walked up close to Sabine. Before leaving, Rich gently brushed her cheek and said,

"Don't take any chances, follow the plan, and if I go down, get the hell out of here."

"Count on me. You have to make it back here, and you will." Rich pulled his binoculars out of his pack and started scoping the area. Suddenly, he spotted the helicopter and the small plane that he had seen parked by the front entrance. "I knew those vehicles had been moved, and now I know where. I will have to take out one of the tires on the plane and disable the chopper with a bullet or two."

"Won't you give yourself away?"

"No, we are using subsonic ammo and silencers that prevent firing flash from being seen. The sound will be no louder than an air gun, don't worry. Rich crawled out of the small gully, and duck walked toward the mound to position himself for the slaughter. As the agent moved forward in the sunlight, the heat and wind burned his face. It was so hot; Rich had to keep wiping off the sweat on his forehead with his cotton shirt sleeve. The adrenaline kicked in as the agent was slowly getting closer and closer to the building. Another five minutes passed before finding a position that would give him a clear shot at the large tiled patio. On the patio's edge stood a humungous black barbecue grill, big enough to cook a steer. Black smoke was rising from the rotisserie. While focusing on the ranch house and patio, Rich took out his walkie-talkie and let Sabine know he was ready to party. Then he told her to go silent.

Rich took his long gun and sighted in the aircraft, a Cessna 182. Then he sighted in the Bell 206 helicopter parked along the runway, both bearing the ranch's emblem. Rich took in a deep breath, then another, and as he exhaled, he slowly squeezed the trigger. The bullet hit just to the left and short of the plane's tire. He readjusted his scope, fired again, and this time was rewarded. A few minutes later, the fired tire went flat, and the Cessna, it seemed, appeared a bit lopsided as the tire went flat. Rich waited quietly to see if anyone busy on the patio would react to his action. He moved his sights on the chopper, fired five times with high impact rounds into the engine block. With that damaging treatment, he figured that the helicopter would not leave the ground. The agent replaced the mag with a full one.

Several minutes later, the patio started to become alive with cooks checking the grill and the Mexican band lining up and tuning their instruments. Helpers were spreading white tablecloths over the two large tables. The musicians, wearing black sombreros and dressed in black suits ornated with silver embroideries on their boleros and pants, were ordered to begin playing mariachis. Attracted by the music or following a signal from their host, the guests, holding a glass of liquor in one hand, appeared on the patio. Smoke from cigars rose into the air along with that from the grill. Rich watched with his binoculars, trying to match the three CEOs' faces to pictures he was carrying in his pocket. He immediately identified Captain Spencer standing by the grill with his rifle on his shoulder.

Then Rich sighted Wilkerson. The agent would be patient and wait until three or four men formed before doing anything. All the time he scoped the bastards, he kept wiping sweat off his face. Just as he was almost ready to shoot one of the men, Captain Spencer walked over to join CEO Rhinegold and someone else turning his back, who may have been Wilkerson. Rich quickly stuffed his binoculars in his small pack and sighted in the first man. He made sure the scope was adjusted, put the crosshairs on the top of Rhinegold's chest, and fired. Within a split second, the man fell, and one could see a red blob appear high on the victim's shirt. Rich moved the scope hairs over to Wilkerson and pulled the trigger once more. Another red spot appeared in the center of the man's head. Immediately, there was panic; men dropped their drinks and began running toward the ranch house. The five musicians disappeared instantly. Taking advantage of the confusion, Rich continued to fire, taking a man down with each shot. The patio became silent and deserted again except for guards with guns appearing out of nowhere. Some were running toward dirt bikes, others toward vehicles.

Rich spotted Captain Spencer giving orders to a group of men. The agent fired, never knowing where he hit him. Spencer went down, and Rich was confident it was forever. Then Rich fired three more rounds into the guards, taking a man down with each bullet. While running back toward Sabine, he changed mags. All of a sudden, Rich was close enough to hear Sabine's Remington barking as round after round flew toward the group.

When he slid into the trench, he informed Sabine he hit eight, and maybe even ten or more. The two partners had to go now.

As they moved back toward their dirt bike, they could hear the roar of speeding motorcycles and see dust flying. Rich sighted in a man on a dirt bike and fired him. Two dirt bikes were moving end over end as two men died before they hit the ground. Then the two partners sighted in a jeep and shot the driver, causing the vehicle to go erratically, out of control. Sabine and Rich turned and ran as fast as they could toward their dirt bike. They could hear automatic fire behind them, the bullets causing the dry dirt to rise into the air all around them. Both Sabine and Rich stopped, knelt, fired, and took out two drivers, immobilizing two more vehicles. Rich pulled off his ceramic oversized bulletproof vest and pulled Sabine's arms through it.

"What the hell are you doing? I am wearing my bulletproof vest."

"You will be sitting behind me on the bike and taking hits. No way will one vest stop some of those high power rounds." With authority, the agent added, "Keep your head low and follow orders." Rich had the bike up and running in less than ten seconds.

The small dirt bike howled as Rich redlined the RPM's. Then all of a sudden, Sabine was hit in the back by a bullet. She violently jerked her chest against Rich's back with much force. Rich knew what happened. She was hit one more time. Rich also felt pressure from her arms as she tried to keep her balance on the bike and cope with the pain. Then he felt something wet on his arm. She was bleeding.

The sun had dropped below the horizon, and it was now dusk. The silence returned. The non-stop roaring of motorcycles and car engines had stopped. Rich parked on the edge of the arroyo. Below, in the ravine, there was semidarkness. Both Rich and injured Sabine remained on the rim of the canyon, alert to any sound.

She was injured but not out of service. A bandage was wrapped over her fatigues to stop the bleeding from her right arm. They rode in the glider's direction back on the dirt bike, and Rich pushed a button on his firing timer.

An explosion occurred far behind them, in the opposite direction. The agent hoped the dust clouds and flames created by the explosion would make the guards pursuit follow the explosives' sound.

After their dangerous escape, they finally reached the glider. Rich put a small napalm bomb on the bike and placed gas cans next to it. There would be no trace of their DNA or other evidence left behind. The couple descended the edge of the arroyo where the glider was parked. Sabine kneeled in a firing position with her gun safety off as Rich prepared the glider for their ride away from their attackers. After the engine fired, she sat down in front of Rich, and he redlined the small engine to get as much thrust from the propeller as he could. As they became airborne, Rich fired another explosive, and then another a minute minutes later to keep the guards going the wrong way. There was only some moonlight as they flew away.

Rich fired off his last explosive and pulled the powered glider up above the ridgeline. Soon, they reached the SUV. The agent made a low pass and sat the flying machine down. Before leaving, he folded the sail of the glider down and put the aircraft on the trailer. All surfaces were soaked with gas. Rich pulled the small napalm grenade pin and threw it in the direction of the trailer. There was a whoosh sound, and then a hot flame engulfed everything. Rich knew there would be no evidence left when he threw a second napalm grenade on the glider, to be sure.

There was a rooster tail of dirt behind the two rear wheels as the SUV sped down the road. In the SUV, Rich had handed Sabine a trauma dressing to put over her wound. As their vehicle sped along he asked her to cut her shirt to take a look at her lesion. From what Rich could see while trying to keep both eyes on the narrow road, the bullet had just made a deep cut as it passed across the arm. Soon they would be on the highway and only a short drive to their other vehicle.

Once on the paved road, Rich maintained the speed limit until he saw the landmark, three fallen trees, letting him know where to turn. The dirt path would lead them to where their second car was parked. After removing their equipment, Rich wiped Sabine's and his rifle with Clorox and threw them in the SUV along with two explosives and another thermal grenade.

Before pulling out onto the highway, they made sure no traffic was coming in either direction. Rich pushed the timer button, and both he and Sabine heard a loud detonation behind them as they drove down the road like two locals on their way home. Two miles before passing the main gate leading into the game ranch, they were overtaken by two fast-moving vehicles with yellow lights flashing. Both bore a sign on the car door that read 'security.' They undoubtedly were heading toward the ranch.

CHAPTER 20

A S THEY DROVE ALONG, THE ONLY LIGHT THAT RICH and Sabine could see was their vehicle headlights. Sabine had remained very quiet. She was holding her injured arm, and once in a while, Rich could hear her faintly moaning from the pain as she changed position on her seat. She had not complained, not wanting to become a nuisance. Suddenly, they saw a police car's red and blue lights fast approaching from the opposite direction, without a doubt heading toward the game ranch. The words Texas Rangers were painted on the side of the vehicle.

Sabine was hurting. Rich was hoping to find a drugstore open to get some local anesthetic and sterile fluid to cleansed and suture her wound. All he had in his small medkit were expired antibiotics, a suture kit, and pain medication. He would have to stop soon to administer the analgesics.

On the battlefield in Afghanistan, Rich remembered being sewed up twice without lidocaine, and damn it hurt. He was sure Sabine could not handle the pain without anesthetics. There were no headlights visible, so Rich pulled over to the side of the road and grabbed his pack on the back seat. He removed the container of #10-325mg

Hydrocodone and the expired bottle of antibiotics. Better than nothing, Rich thought. He handed Sabine a bottle of water, two pain pills, and two antibiotic tablets. He figured he had enough antibiotics for a ten-day treatment.

By the time they reached the outskirts of San Angelo, Sabine was asleep. The agent spotted a small roadside gas station and an open feed store. After turning off his headlights, he parked on the side of the building, changed his fatigues for a pair of jeans and a pullover shirt, put on his cowboy hat and glasses, and stuck a mustache below his nose. To completely change his appearance, he walked with a limp as he entered the store. An older man with a hump on his upper back and an unlit cigarette butt in his mouth's corner came over to wait on him. He said, "Well, son, what you all needing this time of night?" Then the man spat a gob of chewing tobacco into the hay covering the floor.

"I have a big dog back at my campsite that got chewed on by some coyotes. I'm hoping you have something I can deaden the dog's wound with so I can sew up the gashes."

"You know what? I have lidocaine. What size your dog?"

"About a hundred ten pounds. Could you sell me enough antibiotics and a syringe also?"

"Yeh." Then the older man spat some more tobacco and yellow slime. "You will need some special gear, or that dog of yours will chew you up. Come with me to the cold box back there. I have what you need."

Rich started to say he did not need a suture kit but caught himself. The older man advised him to use a good disinfectant to cleanse the wounds. The medications were placed in a sack. "The total is a hundred and twenty-two dollars and ninety cents. He spat another gob of moist yellowish tobacco that landed at Rich's feet. "What do you call that dog of yours, young man?" Rich started to slur his words, and finally said, "Bo. He is like a brother to me." Rich handed the man a hundred and thirty dollars and told him to keep the change. After thanking the older man once more, he said he would drop by on his way back north.

Sabine was still asleep as they were heading toward Dallas. It was just after three a.m. when they pulled in at the Sheraton DFW Airport Hotel. The clerk assigned a room on the second floor. Rich insisted on getting a floor level room as he did not like to be above the ground floor. After mumbling, the clerk sent them to a suite at the back of the hotel. Sure no one was up, Rich carried Sabine into the room and laid her on the bed he had covered with a plastic sheet. She was drowsy and wondering what was happening. He brought in their packs and carry on bag.

Gently, Rich removed his partner's army shirt to free her left arm. The deep cut was located an inch from her shoulder joint. After scrubbing his hands thoroughly, he cleansed the injured area and injected it with the numbing agent. Rich could now see a second bullet wound on her lower arm. This one was superficial and would not require any special treatment, only cleansing and a large band-aid. The agent figured a piece of shrapnel had hit the edge of the vest, bounced off, and then passed along her arm, causing the second wound. Now fully awake, Sabine asked Rich what was going on. "It's time to treat your arm." The whole time Sabine stayed perfectly still while Rich worked with calm and efficiency. To prevent any leakage, he secured the sterile dressing with an elastic bandage. Wearing only her black lace bra, Rich admired her arms' firmness and slimness and could not help evaluating she was probably wearing a 34B bra. With her partner's help, Sabine put on a comfortable sweat top.

After collecting fatigues, bloody clothes, and other items, he wrapped them up in a ball and left them in the tub. Before leaving, Rich administered another Hydrocodone dose, only ten milligrams this time. She had watched him caring for her with kindness; Sabine asked him to sit on her bed before leaving." In a quavering voice, Sabine said, "You have taken good care of me, and I appreciate your patience and the attention I received." She managed to position her injured arm around his neck and bring her head against his chest to thank him. Rich took pleasure in the contact and reciprocated by gently squeezing her upper body. The two partners embraced for a full minute, and this body to body proximity led to an amorous kiss. When they separated, Rich said, "We have been through a lot together, I am starting to fall for you. I truly enjoyed taking care of you; now, you must get back on your feet." Sabine felt relaxed, warm all over, happy. She fell asleep again, and Rich left the hotel to find an all-night store to buy a gallon of bleach to soak the bathroom's clothes. All the discarded garb and the used medical supplies would be thrown away in a commercial garbage bin behind the hotel. Now Rich had to get rid of the car and a few more things; he would do that in the city's high crime section. After wiping down the vehicle, the agent headed for the Walton Walker area, a neighborhood with a bad reputation. Rich would leave the keys inside the car, wipe down his seat, and walk to a safe part of town to catch a cab or thumb a ride back into the city. He planned to try and be back at the hotel before eight a.m. The drive to Walton Walker had taken longer than Rich had anticipated, and getting out of it took even longer. It was just after five am when Rich found a cab, and it was almost nine when he opened the door of the room. Sabine was lying in bed with her injured arm propped up on a pillow, watching television news.

CHAPTER 21

S HE QUIETLY ENTERED, RICH APPROACHED SABINE, his eyes began to water, and small drops appeared on his cheeks. The woman he loved was injured, and most likely in pain. He sat on the bed next to Sabine for a few moments, then leaned over and gently placed his lips on hers and said, "I love you." He knew she was sleep, but he had to let her know. "I need to take a shower, my love, you rest for a little while." Rich turned off the small light next to the bed, not knowing that Sabine was only pretending to be asleep. Though exhausted and in some pain, Sabine could not give in to the dream world of sleep.

After scrubbing himself from head to toe, he turned the water on as hot as he could stand it; then he turned and let it spray his back muscles. The pain became less, tension, and the muscles began to lose their tightness after about five minutes. Rich then turned the water on cold and let it spray him from his head down; he needed to be alert as they had to fly to Washington, DC later in the day.

After drying himself off, he wrapped the towel around his waist and walked back to the bed. Sabine was still asleep, and there seemed to be a smile on her face.

He looked at his watch and realized he had time to sleep for several hours before making transfer and hotel reservations.

As quiet and slow as a church mouse, he slipped in under the white sheets in the nude. He told his inner mind to awaken him in two hours.

Just as was about to give way to the other side, called sleep, he felt something touch the skin of his firm stomach muscles. Then these sensitive whatever worked their way toward his groin. Rich's mind began to focus, and he realized it was fingers; Sabine's for sure. Rich tried to control himself, but the urge that had been there since he had met and worked with this beautiful and intelligent creature gave in.

As the fingers worked magic, he became aroused, something like a snake began to crawl across his legs. Now starting to breathe heavy, he realized it was Sabine's leg. Her fingers walked their way up to his kneck, and then she slid on top of him. As their lips met, and the vipers tongue began to search inside his mouth, she pulled herself up on her knees. She let go with her uninjured hand and placed his manhood in the moist heaven. It was not long before the two reached paradise.

Sabine laid on top of several minutes before she slid off to the side of Rich. Their lips met, and the lovemaking was slow and gentle over the next hour until exhaustion took over the two, who were one were in the dream world.

Rich's biological clock kicked in and slid from covers. After making coffee and sat down at the small table provided. After a few sips of coffee, he reached for his iPhone. He needed to reserve a hotel room in DC and get a flight there for Sabine. As he spoke to the lady on the phone, he wrote the room number for Sabine at the Courtyard Arlington Crystal Hotel. The lady then assured him there was a courtesy van to the hotel. One down, Rich thought to himself. Now he needed to get Sabine a flight to DC. Rich perused his phone options and reserved a first-class flight for her that left at 2:05 pm. After a sigh of relief, he started getting dressed when he heard Sabine moan.

As he checked her bandage, Sabine awakened. "You seem rested, my love, how about crawling in bed with me?"

After kissing her on the forehead, Rich said, "I would love to, but we have to fly out today. It would be best if you got dressed and packed. I can help you if you wish."

Sabine slid to the edge of the bed, kissed her man, and headed for the bathroom. When she returned, Rich gave her a cup of coffee, and they touched and talked. Rich looked at his watch and said, "Sabine, we have to get ready to go."

Rich picked up all his dirty clothes and put them in a plastic bag. Then he picked up the used bandages and other items and placed them in the bag. He did not want to leave anything that someone could get DNA. After checking with Sabine, Rich took the bag outside the hotel to find a dumpster, while Sabine showered and dressed.

Back in their room, the couple wiped off everything they might have touched. As the coupe left, Rich wiped off the doorknob. As they walked through the hotel, Rich made sure no cameras could get a picture of their face.

A s they drove toward the airport, Rich pulled over at a Restaurant.

They had enough time for a good brunch and conversation before Sabine's plane left.

The couple were famished, and there was not much talking until the hunger pangs were satisfied. After going over the plans for the day, Rich said, "Hon, you must remember to use your right arm to pull your luggage. When you get on board the aircraft, do not lift your luggage into the bin; there are men on the plane drooling who will do the work for you."

Sabine laughed and then placed her hand on Rich's. After a few seconds Rich said, "I need to call the FedEx pilot. I need a ride to DC."

Rich once again took his iPhone and made his call. Not much was said as both men knew the drill. After Rich finished his call, he turned to Sabine and said, "I fly out at nine pm. I will rent a car and be at the hotel around nine am. My ride has to make several stops."

Just after 12:30 pm, Rich drove up to the airport entrance terminal.

The couple kissed and hugged like there was no tomorrow before Sabine left with wet eyes into the terminal.

Rich had a long wait and day before his flight left.

CHAPTER 22
Washington DC.

Several hours later.

THE LANDING GEAR MADE AN EXCESSIVE GRINDING loud noise when it dropped and locked into place, causing Rich to awaken. Within two minutes, the big FedEx carrier plane, fully loaded, bounced several times after the tarmac's landing gear. Rich stretched as the aircraft taxied toward its assigned parking space. The big bird came to a full stop; Rich stepped onto the ramp. After filling his lungs with air, he coughed and gagged as he walked on the Reagan international airport's tarmac. The air smelled like fumes, so he placed his handkerchief over his mouth and nose. Looking up into the heavens, the agent noticed that no stars were visible. He remembered when in Texas, the universe twinkled like ice crystals, and one could see forever. Reminding himself not to breathe deeply, he walked to the car rental agency. After the usual dozen papers were signed, he headed for the hotel to be with Sabine. As Rich drove along, all he could see was concrete, blacktop, buildings, and now and then a tree. Looking at his watch, he made a mental note that it was just after one p.m. Rich quietly opened the door of room 157 at the Courtyard Arlington Crystal Hotel. Like a mouse, the agent moved across the room, then sat his pack down and gently removed his shoes and clothes. In the nude, he walked across the room and into the bathroom. The hot water ran across his body, bringing relief from the tension built up over the past week. Smiling, Rich was aware that the calm he experienced was temporary; there would surely be another assignment waiting in the UPS store's rented box. Right now, he needed rest, and he needed to enjoy some time with Sabine, he had come to respect as a good partner, and with whom he was falling in love. Each moment he was with her, he became more attached and wanted to be with her all the time. With no more thinking, Rich toweled himself off, then slipped under the clean white sheets of the king-size bed.

As his head met the pillow, he felt a leg slide over his left leg; then, an arm slid slowly over his shoulder and his firm chest. Two fingers began to rub his nipple tip gently. There was a pause, and now he could feel the wetness of a tongue. His breathing increased. Rich tried to turn but was held firmly in place by a small and warm body. Her sweet-smelling soft hair tickled his face. Rich was sure his pulse was at least one hundred and twenty; he gasped for air with excitement. Then the agile little hand slowly moved along his stiff erection. The pressure was too much, so his muscular body pushed the petite woman gently over on her back. Sabine moaned as her legs spread apart.

Rich kissed her nipples, ran the tip of his fingers around the firm erected nipples. Sabine moaned with pleasure as he kissed her ears' tips and ran his lips along hers, hardly letting his lips touch. Sabine began to squirm, and Rich could feel the desire growing as his leg slipped between hers. There was no stopping them now; Sabine wrapped her arms around Rich's body and pulled him into her. During the night, the lovemaking became less aggressive, more voluptuous; the two lovers wanted to enjoy the pleasure of one loving another.

Rich never awakened until after seven a.m., two hours past his usual time to arise in the morning. The stress of planning the op, carrying it out, and taking other human beings' lives had taken its toll on Rich's body and mind.

Rich made coffee. He took his time enjoying his first cup before pouring one for Sabine, which he set on the nightstand next to her. Looking at her, he realized he had found something missing in his life, love. Sabine reached out for Rich's hand. "Do we have to get up now?"

"I have to go to the UPS store to get my next assignment. If you feel up to it, would you like to go?"

"Let me shower first, then breakfast, and I will be ready for anything," Rich replied.

"After your shower, let me look at your lesions and re-bandage your wounded arm. I will order room service while you clean up. Anything special you want?"

"You order; and make sure you include a pot of coffee, I need a caffeine lift."

The morning seemed to move faster than usual, and it was after ten a.m. when the two partners got on the road. Rich explained to Sabine how to detect if someone is on one's tail. The two drove around for half an hour before Rich pulled into the UPS parking lot. "Please stay here; I will only be a minute."

"A minute is too long," she laughed------ take your time."

Rich opened the lockbox, and sure enough, there was another large brown sealed envelope waiting for him. A note written directly on top of the packet read, Great Job. The young man helping you is now on the CCC kill list with you. Try to make arrangements for me to meet him. Rich slid into the driver's seat and just stared at the brown envelope. Finally, he opened the seal and slid out some papers and a large photo of a man. Attached was a typed page with the address of Tim Johnson and a brief overview of his activities. Then, written in the last paragraph, the Triads killer's identity was an individual assigned to terminate Rich and anyone working with him. Rich looked at the picture; the man was Asian, Japanese.

The agent estimated he was about five feet ten tall. Rich gasped several times while reading about the number of termination jobs that the man had successfully carried out. As Rich continued to read, he noted that both Interpol and the Japanese government had issued warrants for his arrest. The agent turned the photo over; the man's name was Kaori Junki Okada. He was born June 12, 1986, in Osaka, Japan. Kaori was a trained hitman working for the Triads in Japan and was known to have managed numerous hits in Europe. There was no record of any victims in the United States.

Rich read the short biography several times before handing the photo and paper over to Sabine. Her face features changed as she read the perturbing biography of Akada. She studied the picture, reread the letter, and handed them both back too Rich.

"I think we have our work cut out for us. Let me see the picture of Tim Johnson, please." Sabine studied the picture and the biography of Timothy, then handed it back to Rich.

"Maybe we should meet with the colonel before we head to New York; what do you think?"

"I would like that, but we must not give away the fact that I am his daughter." Sabine studied Rich's despondent look and said, "What's wrong?"

Rich looked into Sabine's eyes and said, "That mission is getting too dangerous for you. The CCC group has hired a Triad killer to kill the two of us. Read this note." Rich handed Sabine the brown envelope with the note written on top.

After Sabine read the message, she said, "We have been through a lot together. A threat like this will not stop me. We have to eliminate as many of the scum as we can."

"Are you ready to meet Colonel Andy Coleman, your father?"

Sabine closed her eyes slightly, looked at Rich, and said, "Yes.

Please do not tell him I am his daughter, not yet; give me time. I will let you know when the time has come to approach the subject. For now, we need a good cover story to explain why I am working with you."

Without hesitating, Rich said, "I thought about that on the way over on the plane. I will tell him that you saved my life while chasing Captain John Hornbrook and his thugs. Just follow my lead. The less we say, the better."

Sabine put her hand on top of Rich's and said, "Sounds good, and I know it will work. What are we doing next?"

"I am going to drive by my condo and see if our friends are still watching it. If so, we will head to lunch. I don't want to spoil a beautiful day and a good meal with someone I care about." Rich had almost said the word love but caught himself. He was still concerned and worried about having Sabine involved in the assassination business.

Rich knew that Sabine loved to eat fish, so he headed for Captain White's Seafood restaurant on Wharf St. SW., and he was almost a hundred percent positive none of The CCC killers would be there.

CHAPTER 23

On their way to Captain White's Seafood restaurant, Rich drove by the White House, then over to the Constitution Gardens, where they stopped to take a few steps down the famed boulevard leading to the Capitol building. After driving by the Supreme Court, Rich headed for the restaurant. "As your tour guide, I inform you this is our last stop."

"Good, I am starving." Sabine laughed, then said, "Just kidding. I enjoyed every moment, and it was nice to see the sites in person. I wish we had more time to explore this city."

Where the two assassins and lovers were now seated, they could look out over the river. Their thoughts were a long way from their next assignment. Their hands touched, and their eyes centered on one another. They talked about Sabine's childhood and Rich's and about Paris and places where they would go when Rich's assignments ended. Soon they were brought back to the present when the waiter sat down two Captain White's seafood samplers.

After the waiter poured the chilled Chenin Blanc wine, the two partners dug into the food with gusto. There was some small talk as they enjoyed the delicious meal served in a very swanky romantic decor. An hour and a half later, an empty wine bottle sat near the ice bucket as the waiter moved up close with another bottle resting on his arm. There was a pop, and their glasses filled once again for another toast, this time with champagne. Sabine looked at Rich with a frown on her face. "I wish it could be like this forever, but I know we have a job to do." Rich said, "Before we return to the hotel, I need to drive by my condo. I want to catch CCC men watching the place. I have seen them stalking the apartment several times before. I doubt they are there now."

The meal ended with a dessert that they savored while sharing more conversation. Sabine looked into Rich's eyes and said, "Thank you for the nice lunch, it was tasty, and the white wine excellent." Giggling, she added, "Should we head back to the hotel to make love, or do you want to drive by your condo?"

Rich had not recovered from the multiple lovemaking sessions earlier. "I think we better go past my residence, then call Andy." Rich smiled and put his left hand on top of Sabine's right thigh. Then, he gave her a quick kiss on the cheek.

Before going to their vehicle, Rich took Sabine to the old fishing boat strategically displayed to promote the restaurant's specialty, fish. A few weeks earlier, at this same place, the colonel had dropped the agent's assignment that would take him to Paris, where he would meet Sabine. Rich's romantic revelation moved sabine, who squeezed his hand and laid her head against his chest.

CHAPTER 24

RICH STOPPED TWO BLOCKS FROM HIS CONDO, TURNED to Sabine, and said, "Act natural, always looking forward. If I say there is someone on your right or left, use your peripheral vision to glance, don't turn your head. If someone is watching my place, I will keep going. OK?"

"Don't worry. I will not act as a spy." While speaking, Sabine had put her hand on his thigh and had slowly moved it upward. Rich was quick to respond to the provocation, "Any more of that, and we will head for the nearest dark alley." This riposte brought up a laugh as the alleys looked very spooky. But Sabine responded, "Good idea, alleys are dark and provide the privacy we need."

When Rich was just a half block from his building, he noticed a man sitting in a black Ford Torino parked on the street's right side. He knew the car did not belong in the area, and it was apparent the individual was watching the neighborhood or waiting for someone. "On your right, just up ahead is a black Ford, inside is one of my stalkers on surveillance duty. There is no way we can go to my place safely. Now watch, as I drive around the corner to the left, I am sure we will spot another CCC hired gun." And they did.

Just over a half-hour passed before Rich pulled into a parking lot next to a Burger King. Let's have a cup of coffee while I make contact with Colonel Andy Coleman. As they sipped their coffee, Rich took out a burner phone from his pack. He turned it over to make sure it was one of the phones Andy had given him. As Rich dialed the numbers, he could see Sabine's behavior change. She was excited to meet her father, but at the same time, she was apprehensive. At age twenty-nine, she planned on meeting her father for the first time.

Rich could detect Sabine's nervousness. He took his right hand and let his fingers softly brush her cheek. That was what she needed, reassurance, and to know that someone was there for her. She smiled as Rich spoke into the phone, saying the code words that Andy wanted to hear.

The two men spoke for five minutes, exchanging statements that meant nothing to Sabine. Then Rich suggested dinner, seven p.m. at the French Restaurant where Rich and Andy had met before. The conversation ended when she heard Rich say, "Roger that." He put the phone into his leather jacket side pocket, looked at Sabine, placed his two hands over hers, and said, "We have a dinner date. I have a lot of time to give you a tour of the area, and then we should return to the hotel to clean up for dinner. Are you up to it?"

"I am anxious, worried about this dinner. I am facing a delicate situation, meeting my father for the first time, for which I am not prepared. I wish you would not get too involved as this is very personal."

"Don't worry, just be yourself and let the evening play out. Relax, you do not have to get into the father-daughter thing; this will evolve at its own pace. Let's see what Andy says when he discovers my young partner is not a man but a woman."

As they drove around, Rich told Sabine about the masonic influence in the designing of the city. He mentioned the original planner, Pierre L'Enfant, who came to America from France to fight in the Revolutionary War and later became a city planner for George Washington. The city owes him its original design. Other architects, including Masons, also contributed to the construction of the White House and the Capitol.

Sabine was well aware of Pierre L'Enfant, but being studious, she never interrupted and listened to the informal presentation of her guide. Neither of them noticed that the sun had moved toward the west. It was after five p.m. when Rich decided to return to the hotel.

CHAPTER 25

I T WAS A FEW MINUTES BEFORE SEVEN WHEN RICH AND Sabine walked into the Lafayette Restaurant's dining room. Rich looked for the least exposed section where the light was dim. As he got a circular view of the large room, he spotted the colonel sitting at a table next to an emergency exit. Elegant as usual, the colonel had on gray trousers, a white shirt, no tie, and a navy blue Blazer. A big warm smile appeared on his face as he was genuinely happy to see Rich. At first, he overlooked Sabine, but when he realized she was Rich's guest, his eyes centered on the attractive young woman and discreetly admired her curvy shape. Andy stood up, put his right hand out in front of the agent, and said, "Son, it's good to have you home safe." The two men hugged, then Rich introduced Sabine, "This is Sabine, my partner. The colonel, who was expecting a male partner, adroitly showed no sign of surprise. Rich went on to say, "I doubt I could have fulfilled either mission without her help. This woman can shoot better than me." Andy studied the young woman's facial features, then put his right hand out and said, "It's a pleasure to meet you. I find it hard to believe someone can outshoot Rich. Sit down, let's talk, and eat. Do you like red wine?"

Sabine smiled, and as he had done, she instinctively studied his facial features, his blue eyes still sparkling for a man in his fifties, his masculine square jaws, and his black hair sprinkled with a bit of gray around the ears. "I love red wine, and it will be interesting for me to try some California reds."

After the waiter had come and gone, the two men discussed what had transpired in Paris and Texas. While sipping his wine, Andy could not take his eyes off Sabine. He asked them where they had met and how they had orchestrated the complicated and dangerous op in Texas. Their discussion was so intense that they never saw the waiter bringing their food. At this moment, they all became quiet.

As the trio savored their dinner of steak, fries, and fresh spring green salad, they continued to talk about the critical challenges that Sabine and Rich had fiercely handled at the ranch in Texas.

Andy picked up the bottle of wine, and as he refilled Sabine's glass, he said, "We were interrupted by the waiter, I still do not know how you found each other. I've heard Rich's version on the phone, but there were holes in his account. As he said that, his right index swung, suggesting that Rich and Sabine's encounter was somewhat unusual or mysterious. Then he dropped the issue and asked Sabine, "Are you sure you want to continue on an assassin path?" The question had no equivoque, and even though the demeaning term assassin did not resonate well, it did not disturb pragmatic Sabine.

"It is a job that we must do. I have personal reasons to be involved that I do not want to discuss. When Rich leaves for New York, I would like to be at his side." At this time, Rich felt a need to switch the subject. He gave Sabine a discreet blink of the eye and said, "Colonel, you were in the Balkans during your early years in the Marines. What are your views on the region and its people?" Sabine was glad to hear Rich tackling this subject. It gave her a chance for a personal read on Andy.

"I loved the Balkan countries and their people. Of course, I hate war, but I would not have met that extraordinary someone without the turmoil there."

Here was the opening that Sabine was hoping for. "You probably met other officers and men and women from other nations during your stay there."

"Yes, our country worked with the United Nations that was present in Bosnia. The most exceptional individual I met was a French woman who worked for the UN and with whom I spent some time." There was a pause followed by a sigh. "God, I loved that lady. But the military dictates where and when one must go next."

Sabine was listening with interest to details that were not entirely foreign to her. Her mother had shared with her some facets of her affair with the colonel. Andy, who was now silently reminiscing, was interrupted by Sabine, "That sounds very romantic, colonel. How did this lovely relation evolve?"

"Please, call me Andy."

There was some hesitation; Andy was unsure how much he should share about the liaison he had during his assignment. "Well, I met a young secretary working for the UN. The woman's name was Marguerite Boucher, Margo, as everyone addressed her. She was beautiful, kind, warm, and very compassionate." Andy's sudden travel in time had forgotten his neighbors at the table. His thoughts were now drifting in the past, a past he would have liked to relive. There was silence at the table.

"Margo had long black hair, like yours, same color. I always felt secure with her, and she could make me forget the turmoil present around us. I loved her with all my heart."

"Why didn't you stay in touch with her? Maybe even marry her. It sounds like the two of you were made for each other."

"Oh, I know. I was thinking about asking Marguerite to marry me, and then I got the word I was being transferred. Getting married one day and leaving for a shit hole assignment the next day was not a good situation. I could not do that to her. Of course, I realized years later that we could have kept the flame of passion burning. The circumstances were different then."

Sabine could detect melancholy and sincere regret in the tone of his voice. "A compassionate person, as you describe her, would have accepted the separation, especially knowing that your absence would be temporary."

"You are right. I wished I had married Marguerite. I have never found a woman I could love as I did her, so I never married." Andy paused again. Then he shared another thought, "You can't change the past young lady, that is why it is so important you make the right decisions in the present. By the way, Sabine, you never told me your last name." The situation was developing too fast. Sabine bore her mother's maiden name, Boucher. She was not ready to reveal her parentage with Andy. The setting was not conducive to disclosing such a happy and somewhat tragic event.

To get away from the identity issue, she took a sip of wine, looked at Andy, and said, "This California wine is delicious. Is it a Cabernet?" She had grabbed the bottle and pretended to read the label on the back of the wine bottle. Now Sabine had to take control of the conversation. Desperate, she asked Andy, "Has the CCC attempted a hit on your life yet?"

"No, not yet. The CCC probably feels safer to watch me and hope I slip up and give the group a chance to take Rich down. This next assignment is going to be extremely dangerous. Tim Johnson surely has well-trained guards around him. The CCC has put a five million dollar reward on Rich's head, and they have hired a Triad killer named Kaori Okada to eliminate him. Miss Sabine, I highly recommend you do not get involved in Rich's next assignment."

"I have personal reasons to get involved. An extra set of eyes is critical when going up against the CCC. Sorry, colonel, but I'm in for the long haul."

Andy could not stop staring at Sabine. He could see the same eyes, the forehead, and other facial features identical to Margurite's. "Promise me you will stay out of the shooting matches, at least."

Andy turned to Rich, who had remained quiet, and said, "I received a message from a friend in Italy, his name is Borgono. He informed me that a priest told him that the Vatican is sending a member of The Brothers Of Sain Longinus to assassinate you."

CHAPTER 26

T HERE WAS COMPLETE SILENCE FROM ALL THREE, AND
no one even picked up a wine glass or moved.
Sabine stared at Andy and Rich, then she said,
"I am a non-practicing Catholic and have never heard
of such a saint. Can you tell us something about this
congregation?'

Andy picked up his coffee cup slowly, took a swallow,
then leaned back in his chair. "All the information that I
could get from Borgono was that the group's head answers
to a Cardinal who takes orders from the Pope. The name
Longinus goes back to the time of Jesus. Even on Google,
I could not find much."

"How do we know the information from Borgono has
merit?' Rich moved his eyes from Andy to Sabine, and he
could read doubt on her face.

"I have been friends with Borgono for over thirty
years. I can tell based on his voice on the phone that he
was concerned. Borgono said that this group of assassins
had been deeply involved in dirty work since the fifteenth
century during our short conversation. Their exposure
became relevant during the time of the Templars. Borgono
stated that a Priest told him the Church had been involved

in political assassinations the past two-hundred years. Before he hung up, Borgono said that the Cardinal had approved the Brothers of Saint Longinus's plan to help the CCC group."

"It's not enough we have to worry about a Triad killer, and now a possible killer of the cloth." Rich turned to see Sabine's reaction. Rich wanted more concrete information. "I wish you had names and pictures." Sabine addressed her partner, "It looks like we will have to be extra cautious. Are we still leaving in the morning Rich?"

Before Rich could reply, Andy spoke. "Due to the new threats, maybe we stop now; it does not look safe for you two; you have already hurt the group, maybe that's enough." Andy was sincerely hoping for a consenting agreement.

Sabine just shook her head. "No way, Andy." Rich started to speak, but she interrupted him, "Rich, are we flying to New York?"

"No way. The two of us can drive; one rests while the other drives. We can switch every few hours, non-negotiable." Rich turned and looked at the colonel. "Andy, see if you can get more info on the new assassins."

"Of course, I will. Oh, before I forget. I believe I told you before, but it is worth saying again. The NSA is a forecaster for the CCC." Andy spent five minutes explaining to Sabine the evils of the NSA.

Over the next half hour, the colonel shared events that a friend in the CIA had collected about the Brotherhood. The accounts, although interesting, did not bring any valuable revelations to the partners.

A lot of time had passed when they started eating their Frangipane tart and sipping coffee. When they finished their dessert, the colonel went over the details of the coming operation. It was midnight when, outside the restaurant, the three hugged and wished each other good luck.

CHAPTER 27

THE DRIVE BACK TO THE HOTEL WAS SILENT. AFTER showering, Sabine and Rich packed their clothes and other goods. Rich made sure to put a Sig Sauer under both seats with a bullet in the chamber and the safety off. Rich took the wheel first as he knew the route out of Washington, DC. Since it was a short journey of two hundred and forty-five miles, the agent decided he would change the driving duties with Sabine outside of Philadelphia. After filling their vehicle with gasoline, the two partners used the restrooms and were back on the highway with a coffee cup. Sabine felt relaxed driving; the traffic was light since it was after midnight. On highway 95, just outside of New York, Sabine pulled over to let Rich drive into the city.

Rich had placed Timothy (Tim) Johnson's address in their vehicle's GPS before leaving DC. It was just after six a.m. when they passed Tim's home, and already the traffic was too much for Rich's liking. He asked Sabine to watch Tim's residence as he drove back and forth. Rich said, "We will have to recon the area several times later in the day, for now, we have a general idea of the neighborhood."

Once the two were satisfied with their findings, they located a hotel four blocks away.

Sabine was shocked when she saw how much Rich had to pay for parking. After checking in, the two showered and soon were asleep. Sabine had awakened first. As she pushed back a piece of hair in front of her face, she leaned over to place her lips on Rich's cheek. He was snoring and looked peaceful. Should I awaken him, Sabine thought? Like a cat after a bird, she slipped back between the sheets and was soon asleep once more.

Rich awakened just after one p.m.. Still tired and sweaty, he needed to cool off with a cold shower to revive him. It was time to head for the New York Times newspaper office, Tim's place of employment. There they would follow him as he left for the day. Rich had to make sure he became familiar with the schedule and habits of his hit.

Just after five p.m., Tim left the building. Rich and Sabine soon noticed that he had not one, but two guards accompanying him while walking down the block. One guard stayed close, and the other one led twenty feet in front of Tim. It was not long before the stalked man entered a bistro. Rich sent Sabine inside the restaurant to order a drink and watch Tim. As Sabine started to leave, Rich said, "I will be keeping an eye on the place, don't worry. He wanted to keep an eye on the guards who remained outside the building.

Over an hour and three drinks later, Tim left the cafe with Sabine close behind. There was a moment of panic when, unexpectedly, Tim got into a cab with his two guards. Sabine and Rich immediately hailed a taxi, and

Rich asked the driver to stop when it came close to where Tim lived.

Now facing the building, Rich had Sabine act as a lookout as he searched a way to enter Tim's apartment. Twenty minutes went by, and when he returned, he said, "The only way I can get in is to go up on the roof and, using a rope, and come down over the side of the building. It won't be easy, and I will have to do that after midnight when people and cars are not on the street.

"What role will I be playing?"

"We will get a pair of hand-held walkie-talkies. You will watch the street, and when clear, contact me, and I will drop down to Tim's window edge. The window will be easy to open, and I should not leave a trace. We will be watching and following Tim over the next few days. As soon as we think he is somewhat drunk, that will be the night I go in."

"Have you figured how to make it look like an accident?"

"The report says he has been under a lot of stress since his divorce. I am going to have him hang himself."

"Are you sure you won't need help? Even a small man like Tim will fight."

"I am going to put him to sleep temporarily, slide the noose around his neck, and push the chair away. It should be easy; I think I can do it alone.

It would help if you watched outside to make sure no one sees me snooping around the building. Let me know when you believe I have enough time to leave and scale the wall; I will count on you to contact me."

Over the next two days, the two partners watched Tim come home from work. During the rest of the day, Rich and Sabine became tourists. They went to the Empire State Building the first day and walked around 5th avenue. On the second day, they took a city tour and visited the Museum of fine art. And on Friday morning, they saw the twin towers, and later they went to surveil the bistro where Tim hung out. That night Tim spent over three hours in the small restaurant, and when he left, both Rich and Sabine could tell he was intoxicated.

"This is the night," Let's grab a bite to eat on the way back to our hotel. Do you have a dark or black jacket to wear tonight?"

"No. But there is a shopping mall not far from here, where I can buy a dark sweatshirt."

"Sounds good. The shirt first, food second, then rest. We will go over my plan again while we eat. If you have any questions or thoughts, bring them up. Let's do the job and leave the city tonight."

Sabine looked at Rich then said, "Anywhere but New York. A lot to see and do, but too many cars and people."

"I agree. Back to our man, Tim is well known in this city, and the NYPD will curtain his place off as soon as someone finds the body in the morning." At the restaurant, the agent reviewed his plan. At the same time, they shared an Osso Buco alla Minanese; delicious meat cooked in wine, braised slowly until it is fall-off-the-bone tender. With this superb meal, Rich ordered a good bottle of Poggione Brunello red wine. The hour and a half they intended to stay at the restaurant extended into two hours. It was

Sabine who gave the signal to leave. "It's getting late; let's get going."

After paying the check, the two walked hand in hand with their bodies close together back to their hotel. While Sabine showered, Rich laid out the cotton rope and tied it to unwind with ease. While checking the two small short-range hand-held walkie-talkies, Rich stared into the bathroom door that Sabine had left open. Rich laid the walkie-talkies on the bed and mumbled," God, that woman is beautiful."

"Rich, in a few minutes, can you come and scrub my back,"

"With pleasure." Rich kicked off his shoes; he had more on his mind than scrubbing Sabine's back.

Sabine pushed the shower door open just a wee bit. Sure enough, Rich was getting ready to do what she asked. He slipped inside the large shower with washrag and soap. He pushed his body against hers and scrubbed her back while her now firm nipples rubbed against his chest. Sabine could feel the taut muscles, and this contact excited her. Within no time, they were making love under the warm spray of the shower head.

CHAPTER 28

CLOUDS HUNG LOW OVER THE CITY, CAUSING THE HEAT and humidity to be almost unbearable. A slight wind started blowing, the result of a front moving across the Atlantic. Sabine and Rich were wearing their dark clothes when they left their hotel, and even their Levi jeans were black. Inside the small pack on their backs, they had placed gloves, walkie-talkies, and a different top to change into after completing the job. Sabine had covered her head with a black beanie hat. So as not to leave DNA or other possible evidence, Rich also wore a tight shower cover over his hair held in place by his close-fitting hat. Rich had one more article that Sabine did not carry, a short cotton rope necessary to hang Tim. He had also brought a line he would use to climb onto the roof and descend from it, onto the balcony. His pullover plastic covers for his shoes would leave no prints. Rich looked at his watch; it was almost midnight, time to climb onto the roof and get to work.

After the two partners checked their small communication devices, Rich went up the fire escape leading to the roof. His earbud in his right ear was ready to receive Sabine's directives. Once on top of the building, he laid out his equipment and contacted his partner to make sure they could reach each other. The communication being clear, the agent looked over the roof edge to make sure no one was at their windows. The street was silent. Rich tied off his rope's end, then slowly slid down the exterior wall's side until his feet hit the balcony's rod-iron railing. Now standing motionless on the platform, Rich contacted Sabine, who warned him, "Spotter to Starlight, wait for a minute or two, traffic." He looked in her direction and saw two couples coming down the street. He waited until his partner gave him the signal to proceed. Opening the sliding door required little effort, and soon Rich was inside the apartment where he had to adjust to semi-darkness. By chance, a plug-in night light inside a bathroom gave off enough dim glow to allow Rich to navigate without bumping into furniture. This semi-obscurity made him less visible.

He could discern a dining room area and a kitchen. The flat was quiet. He slowly worked his way into the bedroom, where he found Tim sleeping on his back and snoring. The man who was not wearing any top was small in stature and almost skinny. One thin leg was hanging off the side of the king-size bed. The top sheet and blanket were pushed away, exposing the body dressed in navy blue pajama bottoms. Rich took out a bottle of chloroform and poured some on his handkerchief, which he held over the CCC member's mouth and nose, Timothy Johnson, the Times' specialized editor.

There was no defensive response from the victim, only a small tremor when the sweet-smelling anesthetic reached Tim's nose. He was now deeply asleep. Rich threw the end of the rope over a lacquered stationary joist board found between two rooms. He then brought a hardwood regular kitchen chair, placed it beneath the beam, and sat Tim on it. He pushed the loop over Tim's head and around his neck. Before killing Tim, Rich made sure the victim's fingers had come in contact with the noose, the rope, and the chair's back.

Standing on one of the four tall chairs found around the kitchen dining counter, Rich needed to secure the end of the rope to the joist. Even though Johnson was underweight, it is with an extreme effort that he pulled the line over the beam with Tim now hanging with his feet barely touching the chair. Without a sound, this maneuver had strangulated the CCC member. Back on the floor, Rich pushed the chair over. While Tim dangled unconscious, urine ran down his leg, and soon loose fecal matter dripped on the floor. Using his flashlight, the agent looked around to make sure he had not dropped or left anything behind. He was now ready to go.

"Starlight wants to come down."

"Stand by Starlight. I hear voices. I will call back." It seemed like an eternity before Sabine called Rich back to give him the signal to come down. "Clear to go, Starlight."

Being careful not to forget or break anything, Rich opened the sliding door. Making sure again, no one was present on the street; he grabbed his rope to reach the roof. Once back on top of the building, the agent returned everything in his small backpack and contacted Sabine again to make sure the coast was clear before descending the fire escape.

Leaving the alley, Rich started walking casually down the street as if he lived in the neighborhood.

The two partners were happy the mission was over. As they strolled toward their hotel, Rich got rid of his hanky and emptied the small bottle of chloroform in a drain. They felt relieved and could now relax. Little did they know that someone was parked a half block from their hotel and was awaiting their return.

CHAPTER 29

NSIDE THEIR ROOM, THE COUPLE TOOK OFF THEIR clothes and soaked them in a mixture of bleach and water. They changed their clothes, getting ready for their trip back to DC. After wringing out the wet clothes, they placed them into a plastic bag. As she was opening a window, Sabine said, "The room smells like chlorine. I think we should air the place. This odor may raise a few questions."

"Good idea. By the way, I paid for the next three nights in advance, even though we are leaving today. With the 'Do not disturb' sign on the door, no one will check our room for three days, which will give the smell a chance to disappear. You have been wearing your wig every time we walked through the lobby and me my disguise. Let's wipe this place clean of prints, and make sure we leave nothing in the trash. We will take the stairs to the underground parking. I am confident no one will remember us." After giving one last check, Rich said, "Time to go." They both threw their keys on the bed and left.

Rich stopped Sabine, who was eager to get in the car and said, "Just a minute, I never get in my vehicle without first look for tripwires, explosives, or tracking devices. It takes only a few minutes. Rich did a thorough search with Sabine standing a few feet away. When Rich thought it was safe, he motioned to Sabine to get in. She threw her pack on the car's back seat with Rich's luggage and the plastic bag. Once outside New York, Rich would dispose of the garbage bag.

It was late, Rich said, "Let's get out of Dodge fast." Rich started the engine and pulled backward.

"What or where the heck is Dodge?" Sabine was not familiar with the expression.

"Old cowboy saying. Dodge is in the state of Kansas, in the center of the country. In the nineteenth century, Dodge was considered a frontier town, you know, a cowboy town. Outlaws, crooks would hold up a bank, and someone would shout, "Let's get the hell out of Dodge fast." Rich hit the gas, pulled out, shifted into high, and burned a little rubber.

They were now out of New York City, on the expressway south. After a while on the road, the agent pulled into a roadside cafe and gas station. "I am going to fill the car with gas, then park behind the building. You find us a table so we can watch the front door, and if possible, close to an exit, preferably one opening in the back."

"Yes, sir, my Capitan." Sabine leaned over and kissed Rich on the tip of the nose.

After sitting down, the two ordered enough food for four. During the meal, due to fatigue, there was very little talking. Then Rich broke the silence and said, "We are going to take a short detour. I am going to stop in Philly for a few days. There is a lot to see there, and maybe this deviation will throw a curve in the assassin's plans."

"What do you mean by curve? Do you mean something unexpected, a surprise? Another of your expressions."

"I mean our detour it will trick them, fool them. A curve in baseball is when the pitcher throws the ball towards the batter and catcher, he tries to make it curve. I will explain baseball when we go to our first game. Let's get on the road."

It was late morning when the couple pulled into the city of Philadelphia. Rich found a nice hotel close to the old downtown area, and the couple checked in.

Rich and Sabine would never know how close to being executed they had been just outside of Mount Laurel, some fifteen miles from Philadelphia if they had stayed on the same route back to Washington DC.

CHAPTER 30

T HE FOLLOWING MORNING RICH ORDERED ROOM service. As the couple sipped coffee, he displayed the documents that he had picked up at the UPS box the day before, on the bed farthest from the door. Sabine was deep in thought as she read a brief on the CEO of a Louisiana Oil and Chemical producing kingpin. There was a light tap on the door, Sabine jumped.

"Probably room service," Rich said.

She reached for the door, "Hold it," Rich said. He pulled the nightstand drawer open. With his right hand, Rich reached in and brought out his Glock 40 with a silencer screwed on it. Instinctively Rich grabbed the towel that he had left on the bed after showering and covered the gun he held. He ordered Sabine to open the door, "Open the door and step back behind it."

A man about five foot six with both hands on the pushcart entered. On his head was a small green cap, the hotel chain colors. "Good morning, I have your breakfast order."

Keeping a grip on his Glock under the towel, Rich moved over to his nightstand, picked up a ten-dollar bill, then walked over to thank and tip the young man.

After the waiter left the room, Sabine pushed the door closed and locked it. There was a sigh of relief on both faces as they sat the food on their small round table. They sipped coffee and discussed their options for the next CEO's execution and how they should approach Ruben Fournier. Over an hour had passed before they finished their breakfast. Rich pushed his chair back, walked over to make another pot of coffee."

As the coffee was brewing, Rich pulled on a pair of dark blue Savane Ultimate Performance Chino pants. He then pulled over his head a Micro-Mesh Polo Shirt to match. As he tied his shoestrings, the coffee pot quit gurgling. While filling Sabine's cup, she looked at Rich, and in a teasing way, she said, "Oh, you look handsome. I did not know you had such good taste and such a high esthetics standard.

Rich smiled, kissed her on the forehead, and said, "There is a lot you don't know. Did you find out where our CEO friend Eichenbaum is going to be this week?"

"According to the business program on TV, he will be speaking in Dallas, Texas today, and then he will fly to New Orleans to meet with a group of CEOs from the oil and chemical industries." No one spoke for a few seconds, then Sabine said, "I don't think we have enough time to plan a hit on him in Texas."

"I agree. We need to discuss our plan some more and reach a decision soon. Let's not forget the guards who will surround the members of the CCC. For now, let's pack."

T. en minutes had passed when Sabine said, "What's next, boss? I am ready to go."

"First, we wipe all our prints in the room, and then we can head to the airport. Once there, I will put on my disguise and go to a car rental to get a different car. The paperwork will show Chicago as our final destination. Next, we will look for another hotel."

Almost two hours had passed before the couple checked into a hotel situated across the city from the previous one. In the lobby, Rich glanced at the newspaper stand, one of the publications displayed the picture of an Asian man, and in large prints, the title of the article read:

"Japanese man found dead in his vehicle." Intrigued, Rich bought a copy of the Washington Post, folded it, and put it under his armpit. He picked up his backpack and headed for the elevator with Sabine.

CHAPTER 31
Washington DC

RICH TIPPED THE CABBIE GENEROUSLY AND THANKED him. The couple entered the restaurant and, at their request, were promptly taken to a table close to an exit. To relax after their long road trip back to Washington, Rich ordered a Georges De Latour bottle, a Cabernet Sauvignon. Sabine tasted the wine and said, "You have good taste. How come you knew to select this exceptional wine?" Jokingly she added, "I had no idea you were a connoisseur." Acting humble, Rich explained,

"I got help, consulted the internet while you were showering. The food here is equal to the wine, excellent. Are you ready to order?"

"Give me another five minutes. I want to try something new, something I don't get in France." While deciding what to order, Sabine was discreetly teasing Rich under the table, rubbing her foot on his thigh."

Sabine had chosen an entree that included items she had never seen or tasted before, cornbread stuffing, cranberry sauce, sweet potatoes, and pumpkin pie. Of course, with that came more familiar roasted turkey and mashed potatoes. Her selection surprised Rich, who preferred a ribeye steak with all the trimmings. "You chose a Thanksgiving dinner. Are you certain this is what you want?" Sabine nodded her head, yes.

After the waiter left, Rich furtively looked around to make sure no one suspect was in the room. Then out of the blue, he said, "I love you, Sabine. Please let me finish the op alone. I could not live with myself if something happened to you during this dangerous mission."

"I have felt affection for you since your fiasco at the restaurant on the river in Paris. You must remember, you dumped me and then left for Texas without any explanation. We must complete the mission together; doing it gives me great satisfaction. And who knows, the next operation may be low-risk. Let's not discuss this now. We must live and enjoy this moment together."

Around nine p.m. Sabine was just finishing her pumpkin pie topped with whipping cream, which she discovered was delicious. Rich looked around and noticed many customers had already left the restaurant, so he reached into his pocket, brought out the burner phone that Andy had left for him, and punched in the numbers. On the fourth ring, he heard the words of the man he often thought of as his father, Colonel Andy Coleman. After Rich gave the code words, the colonel said, "Outstanding job in New York, son. I am not sure how you and your partner pulled it off, but the CCC and others accept the demise of Timothy Johnson as a suicide."

"Thank you, sir. I could not have done it without my partner. Has the group been putting any pressure on you?"

"They don't even try to be discreet, they follow me everywhere, and they have my phone tapped. The group has been putting the heat on POTUS to send more troops into Syria, Iraq, and Afghanistan and sell our best armory to the Saudis. They want war. Wars bring hundreds of billions, maybe more, into the pockets of the military arms builders. The people of this country are brain dead, son."

"What more can we do to slow down these developments, colonel?"

"It does not make a difference if the people elect a Democrat or Republican leaders; the result is just more profiteering for the rich. I am hoping an outsider will get elected and try to buck the CCC."

"Remember what happened to Kennedy. Short of a revolution, all we can do is take out some of their hitmen like we are doing. By the way, are you working on your next assignment?"

The question, followed by complete silence. Rich tapped the phone with his finger, thinking the battery was dead, or there was a short. The answer came, "The CCC has directed the CIA to stir up things even more in Venezuela; they want a regime change and the control of the oil. I agree a regime change would be good for the population, but the people should take care of their problem without the interference, the uninvited intrusion of outsiders. What I need to tell you next will have to be said in person. I almost forgot to ask, did you two enjoy your meal at Joe's?"

There was a slight gasp for air, and a pause, before Rich could speak, "How did you know we ate there?"

"I followed the cars that kept changing lane, the one that followed your cab. I was afraid they would put a hit on you. " Rich thanked Andy for his protective action. Then the colonel brought up some information he had already discussed with Rich in the past.

"As I told you before, the CCC works closely with the Vatican, and Kaori Okada works as a church hitman. Have you seen him yet?"

"No." There was silence on the phone, then Rich said, "The Vatican is known to have hired hitmen who are sent to different parts of the world. These individuals take out inconvenient anthropologists and archeologists. These experts must not find artifacts and explore past societies' social and cultural issues, which could contradict the church's dogma. These hired fanatic killers are more of a threat than the CCC, I believe."

There was another pause before the colonel spoke again. "Rich, three groups, run this country, the CCC, the NSA that is a dangerous threat to our liberties," he paused, "And the PAC that controls Congress." Changing the subject, the colonel added, "When you leave the restaurant, you will have to lose those bastards who are following you. I have a lot more to discuss with you in person. Tomorrow morning, let's meet where I took you fishing on the Chesapeake Bay, seven a.m. Maybe you should use your partner as a spotter. I have something to tell you."

"Good idea, colonel, I am sure after what we have been through together, my partner would not hesitate. Goodnight, sir."

Rich told Sabine they had been followed after leaving their hotel. Sabine's expression changed; she looked somewhat concerned. "Rich, we have to eliminate those bastards. As Andy suggested, let me be the spotter. Get me a rifle with a scope, and if anyone comes near you, I will take them down."

"Tomorrow, we are going to meet the colonel in person in a relatively deserted area. If I remember the place correctly, there is nothing there.

"Is there any ground cover?"

"Yes. A lot of maple and fir trees, and of course, brush. We will have to go by my condo to get a rifle." Rich thought for a moment, then said, "Let's go to the hotel. I will leave you there and go to my condo."

"Are you crazy? Who will provide cover for you?"

"They won't be expecting me at the apartment. Don't worry. I will be OK."

With diligence, the couple left the restaurant and rushed to the hotel. Sabine was scrutinizing the streets and the alleys. It was late, and in the darkness, everything appeared calm, free of danger. Once inside the hotel, Rich advised Sabine to relax in the room. He would contact her from the condo. With his disguise in place, he kissed Sabine on the cheek and disappeared.

CHAPTER 32

T was late when the agent arrived at the condo. Instead of entering the apartment through the front door, he chose to enter from the back, away from view. He cut the screen of his bedroom window loose and, with his knife, pried the window open. Rich felt relieved when he landed on the soft carpet of his bedroom. After removing the vent cover, he pulled on a thin rope, and a large and heavy package appeared. Rich selected several items, including a Remington Defense CSR (Concealable sniper rifle bound). He made sure the Night force Optics 5.5- 22 x 56 NXS scope was attached, and the AAC SR-7 Fastach 7.62 silencer screwed on. Then he selected two flash suppressors. The agent pulled on another short rope to retrieve a bag containing three mags and a box of 7.62 NATO rounds. Finally, he reached for his gun cleaning equipment that he kept into the drawer of his nightstand. The agent put everything in his backpack. After screwing the vent cover back on, the agent dropped the pack outside on the ground. He shrugged his shoulders and again forced his body through the window. Rich closed the window and rearranged the damaged screen. As promised, he called Sabine, woke her up from a nap, to let her know that everything was OK.

It was late when Rich gave the coded knock on the Hotel room door. After a brief hug, Rich laid out the sniper rifle on the bed and immediately showed his partner the arm's operational characteristics. Rich had Sabine load all three mags and placed the remaining in the small backpack she would be taking along. While Sabine cleaned the rifle, Rich informed her the scope was sighted in for five hundred yards. After Sabine looked into the scope, he also told her how many klicks were needed for each additional hundred yards to adjust it. Following the instructions, the couple climbed into bed and slept for two hours.

Despite a lack of sleep, both partners looked energetic when they got up to drink their coffee and change into dark pants and jackets. Now on the road, Rich said, "We will have to drive into the inner city for a while to make sure we have no one on our tail. Then we will stop for bottled water and energy bars. Make sure you chamber a round in your sidearm and leave the safety off. I have a feeling our snoopers know we are meeting the colonel."

After six a.m., Rich pulled the car into a wooded area over a mile from the meeting site. Sabine snapped the fold-up rifle together, chambered a round, then removed the mag, and replaced the chambered one bullet. She made sure her sidearm was ready.

Once on the hilltop, Rich saw Andy standing near his vehicle, looking out over the bay. The sun was shining even though there were patches of fog slowly rolling along the water's edge. Rich took out his binoculars to look over the two roads below. It was no surprise when he caught sight of a parked vehicle with a man behind the wheel. "We have company about two-thirds of a mile down the road, on your right. That means one or more guests are hiding somewhere in the trees."

"How come they have not killed the colonel or taken him hostage?"

"They are after me and want me dead. Those bastards have no idea you are here."

As they drove toward the meeting place, there was silence for a while, then Sabine said, "There must be a mole among the President's entourage? How do they know we are here?" Rich shared with Sabine how any phone exchange between citizens can be monitored.

"After 911, within hours, the constitution was gutted, and many of the people's rights were taken away. A plan was already in place to do this before the fall of the towers. The CCC and many others in our government needed a catastrophe to vote The Patriot Act into law. No one even read the paper before voting. The President had carte blanche. One House Representative, Dennis Kucinich, a Democrat, voted no to the passage of this law. Later the Democrats made changes to his voting district so another Democrat could get elected in his place. The two parties are almost the same."

"How can the people of your country let this happen."

"Not everybody approved, but many Americans don't vote, and most are unaware of what is going on in our nation. Plus, the news media is controlled up to a point. Most people are more interested in sports, movie stars, and sensational news than in their rights. The media covers what people want to hear and plays with emotions to maintain the ratings. The result is that after nine-eleven, the number of NSA secret agents multiplied without justification, and that organization was given unaccounted billions of dollars. They have banks after banks of computers in UTAH, taking up space the size of several football fields. There are hundreds of thousands of people being monitored continuously. Remind me later to tell you about the role of the Catholic Church and Religion in our government. We better focus on our assignment as we're getting close to our destination." Rich turned onto a dirt road where the trees and brush formed a canopy over the car."

As he pulled into a clearing, he stopped the car and turned off the engine.

"You see that small hill up ahead?"

"Yes. That is where you want me to give you cover from, right?"

"Yes. I will pull in next to the colonel so our cars will form a V and point outward for a quick getaway. The engine blocks will provide some heavier cover in case there is a shoot out. Remember, if you see a sniper, take him out and roll. They will see your gun flash and fire in your direction. Each time you fire, roll, and fire from a different spot. If things get bad, work your way back to the road and hitch a ride out of here after you dump your arms. That's an order." Rich had to tell her that, but he knew she would never leave him and her father while alive. Rich then pointed to the area where he was sure a sniper or two would be. "Take your weapons and a bottle of water. I will give you twenty minutes to find a hiding place. I am on my way to the water's edge."

CHAPTER 33

BEFORE LEAVING, SABINE PLACED HER COMMUNICATION unit in her ear to test it, and she made sure her sidearm was ready before disappearing into the brush and trees.

The twenty minutes seemed like an eternity as Rich nervously checked his watch at frequent intervals. At twenty minutes, Sabine gave three klicks on her mike to let her partner know she was in place. As Rich pulled back onto the dirt road, he heard her say, "We have company about two-thirds of a mile down the road on your left, almost at the Y. That means one or more guests are hiding somewhere in the trees." Rich clicked his mike to acknowledge and turned toward the water's edge.

The sun was shining bright, but there were still patches of fog along the water's edge. The vehicle he had spotted earlier was now in plain view. It appeared that the older man at the wheel had some tactical experience; his truck pointed outward. Pulling into place, he had left enough room so each vehicle could exit without turning.

Before leaving his car, Rich placed his automatic weapon on the front seat along with three mags. He slid over into the passenger side to exit with the protection of the V formed by the two vehicles. Keeping his back to the door, he greeted the colonel, "Good morning, a nice day for a visit."

"Did you see our company on the way in?"

"My spotter informed me. Sabine is stationed on the hill behind you. Have you seen any signs of our friends anywhere?"

"I was sure I saw the sun reflect from something in the trees about three hundred yards behind you. Not sure, though. Let's talk for a while. In twenty minutes, the sun will expose the area where I think those misfits are hiding. That was the reason I chose to meet you early, and here. The timing was important."

"What's the latest on the CCC?"

"I am sure they have a termination order out on me, either today or when I am out of the public eye. That is why I wanted to meet here. I am hoping your sniper can take them out. Also, I want to give you the name of the NSA mole and the CCC representative who has been meeting with POTUS."

"I presume those individuals are at the center of my next assignment. Who are they?" Just as Andy started to reveal the names, a rifle shot hit him high on the chest's right side. The colonel went down, and as he collapsed, another rifle fired. As he pulled Andy against a vehicle, Rich saw a man fall from a tall fir tree. In the meantime, the colonel's wound was bleeding profusely, soaking through his shirt and windbreaker. Rich leaned forward to place his folded handkerchief on the injury, and with relief, he realized Andy was wearing body armor. "Hang on, colonel. I am going to get you out of here as soon as I can."

There was no answer. Little did Rich know that the bullet had split when it hit the protective vest and a piece had hit the colonel in the head, rendering him unconscious. A second later, a message came on the agent's com unit, "Vehicle heading this way."

Sabine put her scope sight on the head of the driver and fired. Oh shit, she said out loud. The glass of the windshield was bulletproof. She sighted directly into the center of the splintered V on the window and fired again, again, and again. The next message to Rich read, "Tango down, and the vehicle has stopped."

CHAPTER 34

RICH WAS ABOUT TO LET SABINE KNOW THAT ANDY HAD taken a hit, but he was afraid she would instinctively leave her post to see the damage for herself. After all, Andy was her father even though he ignored their close relationship. Instead, Rich ordered her to direct her scope on the right of the tall tree. Rich explained that one of the nemeses had fallen to his death from there."

Sabine widened the vision on her scope, followed Rich's command, and pulled the crosshairs down to the right. A flash was seen before any sound was heard. Almost simultaneously, she fired to the flare's right, and immediately, a fine bloody mist was seen floating in the air. Sabine had hit the shooter in the head. "Tango down."

Rich was worried that the colonel was still not responsive. He asked Sabine to work her way down to the water's edge. "The colonel is wounded. I am sure he will be OK, nothing too serious. I need your help here to control the scene so I can take care of him."

"I am on my way." There was silence on the coms units as Sabine worked her way down the hill. Keeping her head down, her finger ready by the trigger, and her gun pointed forward, she reached the two vehicles just as Andy was regaining consciousness.

His first statement following his recovery was surprising, "The name of the NSA spying is Maxwell Theodore Henderson, he goes by the name of Max. His bio is at the UPS box."

With misty eyes, Sabine knelt next to her father and put her hand under his head. She regretted not having told Andy earlier that he was her father. There would be no more delay; she was ready to share her secret with him.

"I have something to tell you that may turn your world upside down; I am your daughter." The declaration was so abrupt and unexpected that the colonel was temporarily unable to react and remained speechless for a full minute. By then, she was in tears. She had approached her face close to his to kiss him on the forehead. Andy's mind was now clear. "Your mother, is her last name Boucher?"

"Yes, and her first name is Marguerite, my middle name."

"Oh, my God. I had no idea. Your mother never said anything about being pregnant before I left on assignment. Is she OK? Where is she now? Is she married?"

"Mom never married. You left on your assignment the month she found out she was expecting a child. She was never married, dedicated her life to raising me. When she retired, she bought a small cafe in Paris." Following his physical trauma, the colonel was now dealing with an emotional shock, soon followed with a mixture of nostalgia, sadness, and guilt. He became pensive as he squeezed Sabine's hand.

As Andy started to get up, he passed out. Rich, who had stepped aside to give Andy and his daughter some privacy, needed to care for the colonel.

"Sabine, I need you to stand guard so I can patch him up. Now."

Rich had raised his voice to bring Sabine back to the reality of their dangerous situation.

"I need to reinforce his bandage and get him into the rear seat of his vehicle ASAP."

Rich reached into his car and brought out his pack that he laid next to the colonel. He took out QuikClot and some disinfectant. After cleansing the wound, he placed the QickClot into the entry and the exit sites of the lesion located just below the shoulder. There appeared to be no bone or nerve damage. The low bleeding loss seemed to indicate that no vital artery was severed. The head wound was superficial. Rich placed a sterile dressing and bandage on the colonel's head wound and, turning to Sabine, asked, "Do you see anything?"

"Negative, I have a feeling it's time to leave."

"Good. Please give me a hand; we need to lay the colonel in his vehicle's back seat. I'll drive his car, you follow in the other one."

"Are you taking him to a hospital?"

"Negative. Special Ops has a Doctor on retainer. I will make the call. Keep your coms unit on."

Nothing more was said as they placed Andy on the rear seat. Rich checked his vitals signs, turned to Sabine, and put his arms around her. "Your father will be fine. Many times we have been hit worse than this. I am concerned about his head injury, though. After a short hug, Rich said,

"Sorry about the rough voice, but we have to focus in the field, and the last hour your mind seemed to wander. I love you. Now let's go."

Sabine smiled and climbed into the vehicle.

CHAPTER 35

THE WARM SUN HAD LIFTED THE FOG ON THE HORIZON, and a slight breeze was blowing. As the two vehicles pulled around the hill, the trio came across the car Sabine had shot earlier. Steam was coming out from under the hood, and the assassin's lifeless body was still sitting behind the wheel. One could see blood and brain matter all over the splintered windshield. Rich smiled and said out loud, "You got what you deserved, dick head."

"What did you say, son?" The colonel was coming out of his inactive state and was moaning from the back seat.

"Just praising the shooting skills of your daughter, sir."

"How long to the med site?"

"Approximately one hour. Traffic should be light."

Over forty minutes had passed with few words spoken between the two men. Rich contacted his partner, "I am going to be pulling off to the right at the next exit. We will be going into the elite section of the city, where you will see several embassies. The doctor we are going to practices inside a gated area. No one would ever expect he does work for the Black Ops group."

Rich stopped in front of a monumental gate. Then slowly, he entered a set of numbers into a panel on the wall.

The black wrought iron barrier opened inward. The two vehicles pulled through and around a half-circle driveway and stopped at a small quaint looking building adjacent to the doctor's spacious home. A man who looked like the gardener came out with a D-ring stretcher. Few words exchanged as Rich and the man placed Andy onto the canvas.

Inside what looked like a small surgical ward, stood an older man with white hair, dressed in green scrubs. Andy was now on the white sheet of the examination table in the middle of the room.

The old man greeted the patient, "Andy, how nice of you to visit me. What the hell have you done now?" Sabine did not like the doctor's approach; her father needed attention now. She said, "He passed out several times. I think his injuries are serious." The doctor was in no rush, "You kidding me, young lady. This old mule will take more than a little bullet and a scratch on the head to bother him — hell in Afghanistan, he left to go on a twenty-mile hike with worse injuries. Get yourself a drink or some coffee. I will put a bandage on this old fart, and he can go." Since Andy was now conscious and coherent, she left the room to join Rich in the waiting room.

The Doc came closer to Andy and said, "Where did you meet that beautiful lady? She is way too young for you." Andy was becoming impatient, "When are you planning to start the consultation? I am not well." With detectable pride, the colonel added, "The young lady is my daughter."

"Your daughter? As far as I know, you never married."

"Oh, enough, you old butcher. Get me patched up. Get me taken care of, and I will bring you two bottles of the old brandy you like."

One hour later, the Doc came to the waiting room and sat down next to Sabine. "Your father will be fine. I cleaned the wounds and sewed up both bullet holes. I am a little concerned about that piece of cartridge hitting his head. He will have to take it easy for a few days, and if he does not lose consciousness, have headaches, or experience nausea and vomiting, he will be OK." The doctor was intrigued by Andy's daughter; he wanted to know where Andy had met her mother.

"He met my mother in the Balkans." Sabine was brief and abrupt. Her annoyance was so palpable that the doctor immediately gave up digging for more details. She said, "May I go see him?"

"Of course, and if he is steady on his feet, you and Rich can take the old man with you. Here are his pills, two pills, morning and night for the next ten days. Nice to have met you."

Rich figured it would be safer to take the colonel to his condo even though he expected it to be under surveillance. As they drove into his parking space, Rich did not see either one of the two vehicles he spotted before. Rich concluded, "I believe two of the three men we killed today were part of the group watching my home. I still think we need to keep someone on watch, just in case. Is anybody hungry?"

After the colonel had said yes. Sabine said, "I am also. Do you want me to fix something?"

"Just rest, I have frozen pizza and cold beer. Will it be good enough?" After taking Andy to the sofa, Rich headed for the refrigerator.

CHAPTER 36

OVER THE NEXT TWO DAYS, RICH SHOPPED FOR FOOD and household supplies, and Sabine cooked for the trio. The two partners took turns watching for unwanted visitors or anything that looked unusual in the apartment's vicinity. On the morning of the fourth day, all three sat at the kitchen table. Andy looked somber, almost downcast. He spoke in short sentences, all in the first person, "I have done a lot of thinking. I am going to reconnect with Sabine's mother. First, I will contact her, and if she consents to it, I will visit her. Who knows, I may even retire in France. I should have never left the woman I have loved all my adult life. No, I should have never left her." Then, turning to Sabine, he said, "Maybe Sabine can help me by adroitly reintroducing me into her mother's life." After having expressed his sadness and regrets, and his projects to rekindle his relationship with Marguerite, his mood changed.

Feeling full of optimism, he resumed the details concerning the CCC. "Max is the one working for the NSA. The CCC representative is Ruben Bensen Fournier." Jokingly, Rich noted that the individual's last name was French, his first name sounded Jewish, and his middle name was Anglo-American." Andy went over Fournier's background. "This CCC member is a Jew, and his family worked for the Rothschilds, the European banking dynasty so influential in Europe's economic and political history. His middle name is his maternal grandfather's first name. The family's wealth is invested in corporations both in Europe and the States. Hell, six of the wealthiest oligarchs are here in the US, and they are American. Read Ruben's bio; you will learn a lot." No one said anything for almost a minute. Then Andy addressed his daughter, "Sabine, I would rather have you not get involved any further in this high-risk mess, but I know you will, so listen up, you too, Rich. Kaori works for the Vatican. He could very easily get additional men with just one phone call. I have some updated information for you at the UPS box."

"Colonel, I want to finish the job. As you know, Sabine will not stand by and watch." She reinforced her will to remain on the job by adding,

"Damn right, I won't. Rich, you know you would have been killed without my help. Let's finish this together." She got up and walked over to her partner and snuggled against him with one arm around his waist.

"That's what I figured." The colonel said. "Don't take any chances, do what you can. As for me, it will take me a week to get things squared away, and then I will put in for my retirement—enough planning. As you can see, I am fine; I can go back to my apartment. Remember, everything you need to know is at the UPS box. Let's stay in touch. And please, try to finish the job without taking any chances. Remember, Kaori has never left a job unfinished; if you want to quit now, fine with me. The NSA has eyes and ears everywhere. Many individuals are, and many more will be, after your ass."

"We will finish the job, in the meantime, colonel, watch your back." Another half-hour passed before Andy left the parking lot, followed by Rich, who drove away five minutes later and went in circles around his neighborhood to find out that the stalkers had not returned.

At the condo, the two partners loaded their gear and headed for the UPS rental store, where they picked up two large envelopes. They returned to the car to discuss the enclosed documents' contents. Right then, Rich decided to eliminate the CCC member, Ruben Fournier. He figured that taking an NSA representative down first would get the whole legal system after them.

"Where do we find Ruben Fournier?" Sabine asked.

"According to the papers, when in town, he stays in a condo at the Wardman Tower, not far from the White House. His home is in Connecticut."

"I will have Andy ask POTUS if the president has had any contact with Ruben recently. I want you to understand that this guy will have top security, but we should be able to take him down."

"Where to first?"

"The tower."

CHAPTER 37

THE TEMPERATURE WAS IN THE NINETIES WHEN RICH and Sabine drove into a public parking lot adjacent to the tower. The couple had no idea that another vehicle, a black Lincoln with an assassin at the wheel, had pulled in behind them on the far side of the lot. Rich checked his cell phone to go over the weather conditions. The humidity was over seventy percent as the third leg of the mission was about to begin. He advised Sabine to stay away from security devices whenever possible while snooping around. He warned her that Washington DC was like London, bristling with cameras. As Rich toured the area, he soon found an ideal location to monitor the comings and goings of the tenants of this eight-story building. Sabine was to spend her time locating Ruben's apartment.

Two hours had gone by when Rich returned to his vehicle, where Sabine was waiting for him. "You were right; there are cameras inside and outside, everywhere. I found his apartment, number seven-twenty-four, on the seventh floor. He must have a nice unobstructed view of the White House from his place."

"Nothing but the best. Come with me. I found a place where we can have a bite to eat while keeping an eye on the tower. The couple enjoyed a light meal, and a long conversation interrupted by Rich's phone vibrating against his thigh. He took the colonel's call and said, "Your dime."

"You sound mighty jovial; I can tell you are a lot happier than earlier today. Son, listen up, good news."

"Good."

"A few minutes ago, I contacted POTUS to get more information about Ruben. He is scheduled to meet with the president tomorrow afternoon, late. Then, out of curiosity, I stopped in a real estate agency to discuss my eventual condo sale once I retire—nothing official, of course.

Sabine had been listening to the exchange and signaled Rich to let her use his phone. "Colonel, could we have dinner together again? I have had no father for over twenty-some years; now you are talking about leaving again."

"Sorry, I was not thinking. We will meet for dinner tomorrow night, where we celebrated Rich's promotion to Sergeant Major a few years ago." Sabine could hear and feel how excited Andy was while she was expressing her need to be in his company. "Also, inform Rich I dropped the 'P' at the UPS mailbox."

"At what time do we meet?"

"Seven p.m., Virginia time. Rich knows where the restaurant is."

"My father wants to have dinner with us tomorrow night at seven, where you partied when you made Sergeant Major."

"Great southern food."

They were walking back to their car when all of a sudden, Sabine said, "He mentioned the 'P' that he left in your UPS mailbox. What is that?"

"An injectable drug that causes a heart attack and death when overdosed. The CIA and other agencies use it as it's almost impossible to detect."

"Andy said it was at the UPS."

"He's always ahead of us. Let's get our goody, head back to the hotel, and go swimming. What do you think?"

"About time we take a day off." Teasing him, she added, "Anything special in mind for later?"

"Yes, and it won't be that much later."

The couple swam for a while, showered, and returned to their room. Both were tired, and while Rich was darkening the room, Sabine slid under the sheets wearing a girlish nightgown and pulled the white sheet up to her chin. Rich sat down on the corner of the bed, removed his shoes and clothes. Slowly he slid under the fresh, crisp linen. Within seconds Sabine was playing with his hairy chest and nibbling at his ear lobe. Rich ran his hands through Sabine's long hair. Rich gave her a romantic slow, and passionate kiss that immediately resulted in sexual arousal. Their hearts were beating faster as their hands roamed over each other's bodies. In the dark and quiet room, the two lovers started to bring each other pleasure.

After the lovemaking and a short nap, the two sat at the small table to share a beer. Sabine said, "Rich, when we talked with the colonel, he mentioned one of the big oil companies having pipelines or projecting to construct pipelines in the Middle East where the US had troops. I did not hear what he said about Syria."

"Its a long story, but I will make it short. The reason the US went into Iraq was to have control over the oil in the region. Under the next administration, the Secretary of State played a big role in manipulating the US to get involved in northern Syria. Shortly afterward, ISIS became a big player in the Middle East. I believe it was Unocal, the oil company, that wanted to build a gas line across northern Syria to bring natural gas to Europe."

"Syria could benefit from this trade; I don't understand why they would refuse."

"Russia is the chess master in Syria. As you know, Russia sells natural gas to Europe and can dictate its price. Understandably Russia was opposed to this project as the pipeline would cut into its profits. Since Syria refused, the US and its coalition concocted an excuse to take control of Northern Syria. Again, remember, investigative reporters have said that the CIA and the Secretary of State were involved in the upsurge of warriors to fight Syria. This turmoil prevented the existence of a pipeline."

"Why are we fighting the Taliban then?"

"In most foreign policies the CIA is involved in, the foreign country targeted turns against us. Look at what happened in Iran. The US interference resulted in the return to Iran of a radical leader, Ayatollah Khomeini, who stepped in as Iran's supreme leader. Then, of course, the Iranians suffered and still suffer, and most of them hate the US government."

Rich looked at his watch, finished his beer, set the bottle down, and said, "We better clean up and head for the restaurant."

As Sabine was getting dressed, Rich stared at her and could see she was undeniably stunning. Her poise, her natural grace, the way she was able to carry herself in any situation. Though small, her physical strength and athletic abilities allowed her to perform unique and often unsurmountable tasks. To top this off, she had an impressive mind that matched her gorgeous looks.

Rich had been pleasantly admiring the woman he loved. He returned to the present when he felt a soft kiss on the nape of his neck.

CHAPTER 38

The dinner planned by Andy and Sabine lasted over two hours. To introduce a variety of southern food to Sabine, Andy had ordered samples of dishes including fried chicken, collard greens, fried green tomatoes, shrimps, and okra. To conclude this feast, he had chosen sweet stewed fruit, a peach cobbler.

During the meal, the three guests shared their intentions and decisions for the future. Andy, who had been retired from the service for years, could resign his present unspecified assignment at any time now. He planned to free himself very soon to concentrate on his wish to visit Marguerite in the near future. With diplomacy and humbleness, he knew his goal could be accomplished.

Sabine had told him not to rush things, for she did not know how her mother would react since she had been deserted, forgotten, abandoned by the man she loved. Sabine, who was asked by Andy to help him reconquer Marguerite, did not know how to approach her mother sensitively and tactfully. This shocking news about Andy reappearing after thirty years could bring joy or sadness. She spent time mentally rehearsing the manner she would use to announce to her mother that the colonel was alive and wishing to see her. Finally, with apprehension, Sabine found the courage to bring the news to Marguerite, who remained silent on the phone for a full minute.

When she finally responded, she never expressed enthusiasm; she said, "That is quite an unexpected news. I had thirty years to forget Andy. If nothing more, I am glad you met your father. I hope you get a chance to develop a warm relationship with him. After all, he is your dad." Marguerite was too astounded by the situation to express more feelings or to inquire about the colonel. Sabine would let her father know that her mother was now aware of his presence in her life. She planned to strongly advise him not to rush back into her mother's life, but to give her time, reminding him that thirty years of absence would not be easy to forget and forgive."

Meanwhile, at the restaurant, The colonel picked up the bottle of red wine, a Napa Valley Cabernet, and filled all three glasses half full, then sat the bottle down carefully on the white linen table cloth. "My friends, my children, very seldom does one have a second chance at life." There was a pause as he took his white handkerchief from his pocket and dabbed his eyes. "I found love once, lost it, then a young man in the military became an adopted son to me." He stared at Rich and resumed, "Now I find out I have a beautiful daughter. I don't know who has been looking after me up there, but I thank you. I am sure you wondered why I poured your glass half full." Andy looked at the couple, paused, and said, "Well, the other half is the rest of our life to come." He rose and embraced Sabine and Rich with affection.

There were loud klicks as the crystal glasses touched. Then, Colonel Andy Coleman picked up a small briefcase next to his chair and headed to the foyer. There, a man in uniform was waiting to take the colonel to Ronald Regan International airport. He was on his way to put in his resignation from his present assignment.

Rich reached over and squeezed Sabine's hand slightly, leaned forward to whisper in her right ear. "Your father is full of optimism. I hope his dream to rekindle with your mom will come true."

Sabine turned and looked Rich in the eyes and said, "Andy seems to forget that he abandoned my mother at a crucial time. I know her; she was hurt for being rejected without a word. Yes, he is full of optimism, that's good, but he must be cautious how he proceeds. My mother has feelings and pride." Sabine turned to Rich and suggested they go.

Little did the couple know that a big black Tahoe SUV followed them to their hotel.

CHAPTER 39

As Sabine and Rich got out of their vehicle in the underground parking, Rich noticed a black car passing them at high speed. The driver seemed to be oriental. At that moment, the agent felt a strange sensation occurring in his stomach, a sort of sudden warning that had saved his life several times in Afghanistan. Was it Kaori, the contract killer? Rich said, "I think Kaori followed us. Go to our room and stay there. I am going to lead him away and end this once and for all." Sabine immediately replied. "Rich, I can be of use. You have to let me help." Rich said nothing for a short moment, "OK. Get in the car. Take me downtown and park near the tower."

They were almost to the end of the street when a set of headlights pulled out from the underground garage. Neither one spoke as they drove to downtown DC. After parking, the couple walked hand in hand down the street. Approaching a convenience store, Rich noticed an Asian man's reflection in a parked vehicle's side mirror. The assassin was here, and it was time to confront him.

Rich leaned over close to Sabine and said, "The Assassin is behind us. Let's go into that store. Once inside, Rich ordered Sabine to go to the back and get out. Once outside, he told her to hail a cab and go back to the hotel.

Without hesitation, Sabine said, "I can help." Looking stern and sounding irritated, Rich spoke with a firm tone of voice.

"You can help by doing what I said. Kaori won't attack the two of us, and I need to initiate this confrontation to eliminate him. Take a cab, as I said. I do not want any trace of you being with me if something should happen. Now go." Rich saw Sabine's demeanor change. Not once before had Rich seemed so worried or had spoken with such authority. She left.

Leaving the store, Rich lost sight of Kaori. He started walking, passed a dark alley from which a voice shouted, "You stop now. Enter the alley slowly, or I will shoot you." The passage was very dark. According to the sound of the voice, Rich determined that the assassin was not in front of him but to his side. In his peripheral vision, he could see Kaori's outline. The Triad hitman was, standing by a dumpster, holding a knife in his right hand, ready to plunge it in his victim.

And he did, but Rich's reflexes kicked in. His left arm blocked Kaori's right forearm just enough to cause the blade to cut across Rich's left chest. Simultaneously, Rich brought his right foot forward and, with extreme force, hit Kaori's right knee. As the man stumbled, Rich reached down and pulled out a knife attached to his right leg. With his knife still in his hand, Kaori lunged forward again. Rich deeply sliced his opponent's right arm with his Seal Knife. Rick heard Kaori yell something in Japanese as he stumbled backward.

Then Kaori stepped forward and, like a Ninja, leaped into the air and injured Rich's left shoulder while spinning. With his opponent on his knees, Kaori kicked toward Rich's ear. But Rich, anticipating the move, brought his knife up and dug deeply into Kaori's thigh.

The assassin tripped over as he grasped his leg. He was severely wounded and would have to stop the bleeding soon or die. Unable to stand up, Kaori took refuge against the dumpster.

Rich reached for his Sig Sauer gun under his left shoulder and shot the indestructible Triad hitman in the chest.

Ignoring if other executioners would show up, Rich duck walked behind the dumpster for cover. After a full minute, he slowly stood up and looked around; Kaori was gone. The large puddle of blood near the dumpster indicated the agent had sliced one of the killer's arteries. Rich followed the blood trail to the end of the alley and started to wonder how this mysterious disappearance could have taken place with him just a few feet away. The ghost was gone.

Rich's injuries were superficial; his blood loss was minimal, and none had dripped on the pavement. Before leaving the eerie alley, the agent checked for evidence left behind. Satisfied, he started working his way back to where he and Sabine had parked earlier.

CHAPTER 40

T took Rich half an hour to reach his car. Obstinate Sabine had followed orders and had returned to the hotel. At a gas station, Rich cleaned himself the best he could, washed the sweat off his face and, using his handkerchief and a torn strip of cloth from his shirt, applied the improvised pressure bandage over his shoulder cut.

Rich parked his car a block from his hotel. Being careful not to be seen, the agent worked his way through the lobby and took the stairs to his room. He tapped on the hotel door twice, paused, then knocked three times; the signal to let Sabine know it was safe to open the door. As Rich stepped into the warm room, Sabine rushed toward her man. She leaped up, wrapped her legs around Rich's waist, then laid her head on his neck. "Gee, am I happy to see you." Sabine spotted the fresh blood when the agent took off his jacket. "Oh, my God, you have been hit. Why didn't you say something?" She realized her cavalier behavior to welcome Rich had probably caused severe pain due to the injuries.

"It's nothing, don't worry. I severely injured Kaori, but I have no idea where he is. He just mysteriously disappeared

"

in thin air. We will have to pack and move to another hotel in the morning."

"Everything is packed. Let me see your wound."

"It's just a knife scratch. I will wash it off, put a bandage on the shoulder and leave the chest scrape alone, and then go to bed."

"No, you won't." Sabine helped Rich's expose his left shoulder. "It is more than a scratch; you need stitches."

"No, I will clean it, apply a clean dressing, and tape it tight. You can sew it up later. I hope you know how to sew." Rich showed his teeth, and sarcastically laughed silently. Sabine was in no mood to be teased; she quickly took her revenge by showing off, offering him a choice of suturing techniques, "What will it be, the interrupted, or the continuous suture pattern?"

Sabine left a few minutes to get the pack with the supplies. Over one hour passed before Sabine finished suturing Rich's shoulder lesion.

CHAPTER 41

THE FOLLOWING MORNING RICH ordered room service. As the couple sipped coffee, he displayed the documents he had picked up at the UPS box the day before. Sabine was deep in thought as she read a brief on the CEO of an oil and chemical producing operation in Louisiana. There was a light tap on the door, Sabine jumped, but Rich remained calm, "Probably our bacon and eggs."

Reassured, Sabine reached for the door, but Rich intervened, he whispered, "Hold it," and shook his head. He quietly pulled the nightstand drawer open. With his right hand, Rich reached in and brought out his Glock 40 with a silencer screwed on. The agent asked Sabine to open the door and step back behind it.

A man about five foot six was standing there with his hands on a breakfast cart. On his head was a small green cap, part of the hotel chain's uniform. "Good morning, I have your breakfast order."

Keeping a grip on his Glock that he had concealed under a towel, Rich moved over to his nightstand, picked up a ten-dollar bill, then walked over to the young man. Sabine pushed the door closed and locked it. There was a sigh of relief on both faces as they sat the food on their small round table.

While enjoying a copious breakfast, the partners discussed their options to eliminate Ruben Fournier. An hour later, Rich pushed his chair back, walked over to the mini kitchen to make more coffee. Waiting for the brew, he pulled on a pair of dark blue Savane stretch Chino pants and a black polo shirt. As he tied his shoestrings, the coffee pot quit gurgling. While filling Sabine's cup, she looked at Rich with admiration and said, "You are a handsome looking man, I like your attire. You better not get yourself killed, I want to have a few decades loving you."

Rich smiled, kissed her on the forehead, and said, "I have too much to live for to take risks. Did you find out where our CEO Eichenbaum is going to be this week?"

"According to the business show on TV, he will be speaking in Dallas, Texas today, and then he will fly to New Orleans to meet with a group of chief executive officers from the oil and chemical industries meeting there." The time factor was an unsurmountable obstacle for the two partners; no one spoke for a few seconds. Sabine said, "I don't think we have enough time to plan a Texas trip."

"I agree. We need to modify and even postpone our plans and wait for another opportunity when they get together. When those high ranking individuals get around, utmost security is in place. Guards are present in large numbers and circulate incognito on the premises, making our work more complicated. Well, let's start moving. First, let's lay everything on the bed. Then, we wipe all surfaces in the room and the rented car, and then we pack. When all is done, we head to the airport, where we will return our vehicle. I will put on my disguise to match a different driver's license and rent another car in another car rental agency. I will show Chicago as our final destination.

Two hours later, the couple checked into a hotel across the city, far from the previous one. In the lobby, Rich glanced at the newspapers on the stand, one of them, The In-Tower, showed the picture of an Asian man on the front page. Rich recognized the individual in the photo; it was Kaori. The caption read 'Dead Japanese found in his car.' Rich purchased the newspaper and moved on, eager to get to the room to read the article.

CHAPTER 42

Sabine unpacked while Rich read the article about Kaori, the Asian individual mentioned in The In-Towner publication. The agent was not surprised to find out that the man he was to eliminate had bled to death from his knife wound and gunshot in the chest. Rich laughed out loud when he read the identity of the individual, Harato Yamamoto.

"What are you laughing about?"

"The newspaper article. Someone found Kaori dead in his car. He was stabbed and left to die." Sabine had to comment,

"One less scumbag in the world. Must be a big relief for you."

"For sure, but we still have to watch our backs. What's funny is the name, Yamamoto. I know that it is an alias. We will have to celebrate his demise tonight."

"I am still in the dark regarding Ruben Fournier?"

"In a little while, when it's not so bright outside. If the circumstances are favorable, we may even consider getting our man today."

The couple watched television for a while. Then Rich decided it was time to go, "Let's go. Who knows, we might

get lucky and have an opportunity to give him his shot."
While Rich showered, Sabine finished hanging her clothes.

Rich shook the vial of Propofol and prefilled two syringes with the opaque fluid that resembles milk.

"So that is the mystery 'P' mentioned earlier?"

"Yes. The CIA and others have used Propofol for decades to induce heart attacks. It is a strong sedative used for general anesthesia, works fast when given intravenously." They picked up their sidearms, and Rich grabbed the small case containing the two syringes of Propofol. They were now ready. Rich reminded Sabine to be alert around surveillance cameras."

It was evening when the couple arrived at the tower. The last rays of the sun gleamed off Ruben's building and adjacent structures. Rich was not sure Sabine should be involved in eliminating Ruben; he felt this project was delicate and exposed her to too much risk. "Are you all set?" he asked.

"You bet."

"I worry about someone getting a picture of you and tracing you back to your own country. Your wig and disguise are perfect, but you need more transformation. Why don't you go ahead and change your appearance by applying some cosmetics?" Using the rearview mirror, she applied bright red lipstick and modified her eyebrows' shape and color. Rich quickly changed his shirt, put on an old-looking ball cap, and a different pair of dark glasses. The alteration was stunning; just a few simple changes had made them look entirely different and unrecognizable.

It was now six at night. If Ruben were planning to go out for dinner, he would be stepping out of his tower apartment any minute now. The partners decided to hang out by a pool to continue watching the building's main exit."

"Under what conditions are you going to inject that Propofol?"

"Injecting the drug has to be done in the right setting, and sometimes, the best surroundings for this tricky procedure is a crowd where people are packed like sardines. Once injected, the medicine works fast. After receiving an overdose of this potent drug, Ruben will grab his chest due to pain caused by respiratory depression, a lack of oxygen. He will be having a heart attack and will drop to the ground while the killer, incognito, will calmly walk away." Rich stopped speaking, stepped closer to Sabine, and said, "Speaking of the victim, don't turn, but he just came out of his building."

Ruben was now walking down the street. Meanwhile, always keeping an eye for cameras, Sabine and Rich separated while continuing following their prey. Three blocks later, Ruben walked into a pub. The partners were now back together, right behind their man. Before entering the bar, they stepped a few feet away.

"Everything will take place in a split second." Sabine put her right-hand palm up toward Rich. "I have an idea. I should do it. No one would expect a woman to do something like this in such an open public place; after all, ninety percent of murders in the United States are committed by males." Rich was hesitant; he looked at her, held his hand over his mouth, thinking. He made sure the small plastic red caps covered the needles firmly then handed the two syringes to Sabine without a word.

"The second one is just in case you drop one. Get directly behind Ruben and jab him in the buttocks and push the plunger down all the way. At first, he will think one of those around him pinched him. Leave the place nonchalantly, turn left, and go down the alley. I will be waiting. Again, are you sure you want to do this?" "Yes, I am sure." They hugged in the sultry darkness of the dark alley.

As predicted, the bar's lighting was dim. The place was packed and noisy, the perfect setting. To reach the bar demanded a few contortions from the patrons.

On the street, the sun had set. Sabine entered the "Makers and Shakers" pub casually as a regular customer and worked her way closer to couples that Ruben had joined. No one noticed Sabine, who pretended to be aiming for the restroom. She walked by customers without pushing anyone, cautious not to get others' attention. She was getting closer to Ruben. As she was moving in his direction, she placed a syringe in her right hand. The deal maker for the CCC and his group of friends stood by the counter. All of them seemed to be talking at the same time, producing a deafening cacophony. Sabine pulled off he little red plastic cover from the syringe and dropped it in her pocket; the needle was now bare, ready to jab Ruben's right buttock. It was over in a split second. As planned, the victim received his overdose of Propofol. Sabine saw Ruben spilling his drink as he suddenly reached for his butt. Around him, no one paid much attention to the scene.

Sabine calmly moved along toward the front door. She was stepping out when she heard someone yell at one of the bartenders, "Call 911, someone passed out."

She left the premises as more patrons were entering the popular bar. As planned, she turned left and met Rich at the end of the alley. The ambulance siren could be heard in the distance. Sabine sighed, glad the operation was over. She was eager to tell Rich how she had accomplished her objective. Her partner never said much, but she knew he was proud of her.

Once back in their hotel room, Sabine soaked their clothes in bleach and bagged them in a plastic bag, which they discarded two blocks from their hotel. When the lid closed on the dumpster, the two partners felt relieved.

CHAPTER 43

THE COUPLE LEFT THEIR HOTEL EARLY THE FOLLOWING morning. They had a long drive ahead of them, over one thousand miles from Washington DC to New Orleans. Rich figured it would take about sixteen hours. He wanted to get there about midnight, and no later than one a.m. the following morning.

In Atlanta, Georgia, they turned in their vehicle at the airport, then rented another car. During the drive through Mississippi, Sabine asked Rich to give her some information about their next and last assignment, eliminating Simeon Amir Eichenbaum. They knew the task would be difficult, as Andy had provided very little information.

Two hours later, while Rich was driving, Sabine booked a hotel in New Orleans. She turned to Rich and said, "We will be staying at the Hilton New Orleans Hotel situated about half a mile from Bourbon Street in the Central Business District." With a big smile, she added, "Best of all, the hotel is only half a mile from the famous French Quarter and World Trade Center. We will be able to enjoy music at world-famous jazz clubs and, of course, concoct a plan for Eichenbaum's demise."

"Sounds superb. I enjoy jazz once in a while."

"I love jazz also, one hour at a time."

There was silence for a few minutes, then Sabine said, "When we were at the Hotel in Washington DC, you started to tell me about the gold the Nazis stored in Switzerland and Italy. If you are not too tired, could you give me the rest of the information?"

"During the war, the Nazis melted the looted gold from the countries they invaded. Hitler had one of his Generals sign a treaty with Switzerland to store this gold in this country since it was neutral. The gold remained there until the State of Israel went to the World Court and sued to get it back."

"Was there a lot?"

"It has been estimated there were several tons. Gold was about $30.00 to $35.00 an ounce back then. As a result of the suit, Switzerland returned about 1.2 billion dollars to Israel. That sum was nowhere close to what the Germans had deposited in the Swiss banks for safekeeping. Of course, gold is over $1,700.00 an oz now. When it comes to money, trust no one, there is no honesty."

There was silence for several minutes before Sabine continued. "What about the gold the Germans stored in Italy."

"The Nazis made a deal with the catholic church. The Vatican would secure gold and work with them. As soon as the Americans invaded Italy, the Lord's house changed sides and kept the millions of dollars in gold, the German generals had stored there. The church never returned any to Israel. The catholic church is very wealthy, and no one knows what it is worth."

Sabine quickly replied. "I have read investigative reports claiming that the Vatican Bank launders money for the mob."

The two travelers kept quiet the next twenty miles until Rich pulled into a roadside rest so the couple could stretch their legs.

As they continued their drive toward New Orleans, Rich said, "The US has another problem, its lobbyists. These groups buy influence from both parties. For example, Israel pays monies to both parties and gets just about everything they want from Congress. Another influential group is Saudi Arabia. We have laws to ensure we do not sell our strategic arms and other assets to this foreign country. The house of Saud gets all the latest technologies and uses it against their enemies. The Saudis have destroyed Yemen and caused wide famine and destruction there using US arms. Like I said before, on specific issues, money talks and bull shit walks. It makes no difference whether the leading party is democrat or republican, in the swamp, at the white house, the members will sell their souls for the all mighty dollar." Rich was breathing faster as the words flowed like water. He hated corruption and the wars fought to protect the wealth of some at the expense of soldiers and civilians, the victims. Sabine jokingly stated, "Calm down, Rich; you are starting to hyperventilate."

Rich started to laugh at himself and said, "Let's change the subject as I take it personally when I talk about those leeches in Congress." Sabine noted Rich was clenching his teeth, unable not to think about the subject. "Something still bothering you?"

"Yes. The house of Saud is worth trillions of dollars. As for the Jews, their money buys millions of subscriptions to influential newspapers. They buy them so the press won't investigate and write anything derogatory about the state of Israel. It is just a way to buy silence from the news service. The 911 report exposed a lot, then it was blacked out, and the members had to sign non-disclosure waivers. The corruption at the Federal level in our great country is overwhelming, and it makes me sick. We send our children to die for these thieves and liars. The people cheer and believe everything told by Congress."

Sabine leaned over, kissed Rich on the cheek, then began to massage his shoulder.

In New Orleans, Rich stopped, and the partners put on their disguise before entering the hotel where they reserved and paid for two nights.

The next day Rich woke up at five a.m. Contrary to his routine, he stayed in bed until nine a.m. They left for breakfast that was being served in the hotel cozy dining room decorated with a special touch, white linen table cloths, and showy orchids in full bloom with their disguise in place.

After breakfast, they walked across Canal Street and down Rampart Street. They strolled, taking their time to look at the shops until they reached the corner of Bienville Street. There, Rich stopped and said, "If one turns left here and goes a block down to Bourbon Street, one arrives at 209 Bourbon Street where the Galatoires restaurant is situated, and where the group we are chasing will be meeting. It is where we will encounter Simeon Eichenbaum. I think we should go by the Galatoires later, look over the place. Right now le's walk over to the Saint Louis Cathedral. and look for a place to eat."

"Before we do anything else, maybe we should sit on a bench in the park facing the church; it is so pleasant today, no humidity, a soft breeze, and music in the distance. How can you have lunch so soon?"

"You are right, let's do that. In the cathedral square, there are street dancers, acrobats, and mimes. If you want, after our late lunch, let's go to the museum and back here to watch the street show which goes on all day."

The couple had Cajun food, gumbo, and fried catfish seasoned to perfection. After dinner, they strolled down Bourbon Street once more. As they walked by the Galatoires restaurant, Rich spotted the top of a building from which he could assassinate Simeon Eichenbaum. He turned to Sabine and said, "Look, if you raise your head, you can see a balcony with wrought iron railings, the one with all the plants. I can get on top of that building; this spot may be ideal for getting a good view of the restaurant's patrons.

As they strolled up French street, Sabine discreetly looked again at the roof above the balcony and agreed with Rich's hunting station choice. "What weapons are we taking along?"

"We will both take fold up rifles, non-traceable. I will take the first shot through the glass; you will fire immediately after me. Let's see if the building has a fire escape leading to the roof."

The couple turned right into a narrow dark alley, and as they stepped into the dim light, they spotted a steel pull-down wrought iron ladder mounted outside the building. "Looks like we are in luck."

Before heading back to the hotel, they walked the length of Royal and Chartres streets to tentatively figure out their escape route in preparation for the operation scheduled late the following evening.

"I feel tired like I walked twenty miles. It must be because of the long drive we had getting here."

Sleep came early for the couple that night.

CHAPTER 44

New Orleans

IT WAS JUST PAST SEVEN A.M. WHEN RICH SLIPPED OUT of bed. It was late for him, who usually got up no later than five a.m. While the in-room coffee was brewing, Rich showered. As he steps out of the bathroom, Sabine handed him a coffee cup and said, "I was exhausted. I slept like a rock."

After a peck on her cheek, Rich took a sip of the hot brew and said, "It's been tiring

times the last few days. After we pack, are we going downstairs for breakfast?"

"Yes. Let's eat here before leaving. By the way, should I go online and reserve my seat back to Paris?

"Yes, and since you have an open dated ended ticket for your return, you should have no problem. I will give you one of the alias credit cards just in case the plane is full, and you have to find a different carrier. It will take us close to eight hours to drive to Dallas." Rich thought for a moment then said, "I would try and get a flight around nine or ten a.m. if they have one. We should be leaving New Orleans by eleven p.m. if everything goes according to plan." They would drive to Dallas, Sabine would fly to Paris, but Rich was still unsure when he would join her.

"You still have not told me when and how you are going to get to Paris?" Rich replied, "I have connections in Dallas. I might fly to Paris from there or from another city. I will let you know my flight number and time of arrival as soon as I can. In the meantime, we have to make sure no one knows we were together in New Orleans or Dallas. I might even fly out of Dallas later the same day you leave or the following morning."

The couple took their time eating breakfast. Once back in the room, Rich reached into his pack and brought out the fold-up Dragunov sniper rifle chambered for 7.62 x 54MMR and the fold-up AR-15. Both weapons were not registered and were untraceable. He cleaned the guns and went over the operating procedures for the AR15 with Sabine. Once Sabine became familiar with the AR, Rich wiped each bullet for fingerprints, put them in their mags, and slammed them into the rifles. Then he folded up the guns and put them back in his pack.

In preparation for the last phase of their operation, Rich gathered thin raincoats and pants that would cover their bodies and plastic covers for their hair and shoes. He also put in ties to cinch their protective covering tight to their bodies. He did not want to take any chance of leaving DNA behind. The couple went over the remainder of their gear, then set the bags near the front door.

After wiping off all their prints in the room, they left quietly for their vehicle. Out of camera range, Rich switched the license plates on their car. They pulled out and headed toward the French Quarter, and parked near the

Musee Conti wax museum. After a short visit there, they walked on the opposite side of the Galatoires restaurant. As already confirmed the day before, the eating place's front window gave the couple a clear view of the patrons inside. They walked several more streets, turned right, and then came back to the restaurant.

Rich and Sabine, walking arm in arm like an ordinary couple, pretended to do some window shopping, then suddenly, when no one was looking, they made a sharp turn and slipped into a narrow dark alley.

Rich checked the old pull-down escape ladder one last time. It looked sturdy, so he lifted Sabine to help her reach the bottom rung to pull the ladder down, which extended almost to the ground. Sabine returned on the street at the end of the alley and watched for pedestrians. The place being quiet, she gave Rich the signal to climb on the roof. Now on top of the building opposite the restaurant, Rich had a good perspective that allowed him to visualize almost the entire dining room. From his mirador, he tried to estimate time and distance.

Rich reached Sabine on the small headset they had brought with them and asked if it was clear to come down. Together once more, Rich gave her a sitrep of the situation. Nonchalantly, hey continued their walk toward their vehicle.

Since it was after one p.m., Rich suggested they stop at Antoine's for lunch. Sabine was impressed when she discovered this special place's sophisticated decor that opened in 1840, the oldest restaurant in New Orleans. She did not feel her clothes matched this elegant eating place and was secretly hoping the maître d' would tell them a reservation was required.

Following lunch, the couple moved their car over to the opposite of the park, walked half a mile to Saint Louis Cemetary No. 1, and joined a guided tour of the city's oldest cemetery. Later, they worked their way to Jackson Square and watched street artists from a bench before going to the French Market.

After seven p.m., the couple moved their car for the last time and parked it at the corner of Burgundy and Iberville Streets.

Rich was sure the cops would curtain off the Bourbon Street area as soon as someone called in the shooting. The police's standard procedure would be to shut down the streets in a five-block radius from the crime scene. Their car would be parked just outside the barricaded site, and all they would have to do is go down Canal Street, turn left on Claiborne and work their way out onto highway 90 west, on their way to Texas. Rich felt confident the plan was stable and was sure they would be out of New Orleans without any problems after the assassination.

CHAPTER 45

THE STREETS WERE CROWDED AS SABINE AND RICH worked their way down Bourbon Street. They followed the flow, past their destination. Rich looked at his watch and said, "It is almost eight p.m., the guest should be arriving soon." Arm in arm, they made a sharp right turn, stopped, and when no one was present, they slipped in the alley.

With the protection of darkness, Rich and Sabine pulled on their lightweight rain gear and tied off the ends around their wrists and ankles. They pulled rubber covers over their shoes and adjusted their shower caps and hoods. With his gloves on, Rich pulled down the old ladder that had slightly retracted.

Once Sabine reached the top of the building, Rich ascended the ladder. They stooped over and worked their way across the roof edge above Bourbon Street. Sabine put her lips close to Rich's ear and said, "They sure know how to party here, do you hear the noise coming from the street below? It is almost deafening." "During Mardi Gras, the noise is a lot worse."

Safely hidden from the street's traffic, Rich took out the guns from his pack and reconnected them. Then he screwed in place the sound-reducing and flash-suppressors and put a round in each chamber of the rifles. After setting the safety, he handed the AR15 to Sabine and said, "Safety on."

Rich looked at his watch again and said, "It's getting late; they should be arriving."

Within minutes the couple observed several men dressed in ties and suits coming down Bourbon Street. Rich whispered into Sabine's ear, "Have you noticed, they have almost as many guards as the President would have. I spotted six for the lead group. We better make our shots count and hit the road."

With their binoculars, the couple spotted CEO Eichenbaum and two CCC members approaching the diner with two guards preceding them. Closely behind the small delegation, the couple observed more guards. As Rich kept watching, he observed two other guards crossing the street; they would remain posted there the rest of the evening.

Sabine leaned next to Rich and said, "Maybe we should take the shot while the targets are outside the eatery."

"You might be right. If some guards go inside to check out the premises, we can take Eichenbaum down. The CEOs gathered on the sidewalk adjacent to the restaurant, among them was Eichenbaum. They were standing there, conversing with animation. As the group was waiting, Rich whispered, "Let's take him down when I count down to one. I will take one more CEO, the one closest to him, on his right. Then aim for the third one. Once done, drop your gun, and duck walk back to the ladder fast."

"Roger that." Sabine pushed the safety off on her AR15.

Rich also pushed his safety off and said, "Three, two, one."

Two bullets hit Eichenbaum almost simultaneously. Sabine's round hit him just below the kneck, tearing out part of his spine as the shot came out the back. Rick's bullet hit the man in the forehead, removing most of the man's frontal bone and eye sockets. Rich fired once, then twice, taking down another CEO and a guard while Sabine turned right and took the third CEO down.

The couple left their long guns on the rooftop and hustled back to where the ladder was. They could hear screaming and footsteps as they descended the ladder. Once on the ground, they hastily removed their rain gear, head and shoe covers, and put them in Rich's pack. Hand in hand, the couple hurried down the street, mingling with those running away from the scene. Others, of course, froze in place, eager to see what was causing all the confusion.

Once they reached their vehicle, Rich threw the pack on the back seat and immediately started the car. Flashing red and blue lights and screaming sirens appeared from all directions as the authors of the chaos were comfortably driving through the downtown traffic, away from the French Quarter.

CHAPTER 46

ONE COULD FEEL THE TENSION INSIDE THE CAR AS RICH drove through New Orleans. Once on Highway 10, the couple began to relax, and Sabine asked, "How long to Houston?"

"If no problem, about five and a half hours. Watch for a roadside rest. I want to stop at the second one and dispose of a few items."

There was mostly silence as the couple was getting farther from the city. Rich was careful never to exceed the speed limit. Over two hours had passed before Sabine yelled. "The second rest stop is coming up."

Rich pulled over and parked in a dark area away from other cars. When the couple got out of their vehicle, the humidity hit them like a hot shower spray. After Sabine had commented on the moisture in the air, Rich said, "It gets worse as the sun rises, and the further you drive into Texas."

While Sabine stretched her legs, Rich used Clorox to rinse several items and dispose of them in a bag he weighed down with rocks. He threw out the evidence into the waters of a swamp that bordered the rest stop. Sabine took over the driving.

Two hours outside of Houston, the couple pulled over for breakfast at a roadside service center. Before entering, Rich made sure no cameras were recording the coming and going of customers. He went inside and ordered two breakfasts to go. He wanted to make sure Sabine was not seen with him or traced to being in the area.

After five am, the golden rays of the sun appeared in their rearview mirror. When Rich pulled into the Houston International airport, Sabine said, "Why are we stopping here?"

I am going to rent a vehicle one way to Dallas. Once we are in Dallas, I will turn in the car, and we will catch separate cabs to the airport." Rich watched Sabine's face for her reaction, and since there was none, he spoke.

"I have decided to take a later plane to Paris. You fly out first, and I will take the late flight. Do you think it's a good idea?"

Knowing he would fly to France, Sabine expressed her joy, "Yes, it is a good idea. I was so worried about going back to Paris alone. Thoughts ran through my head that you might not come, or you might get arrested." She reached over and ran her fingertips slowly down the side of Rich's face. "Thank you."

All of a sudden red and blue lights appeared behind them. Rich said, "Oh, shit. what now?" Sabine's face was turning pale as she turned slightly in her seat. The police car sped on. One could feel the relief in the vehicle. A few minutes later, the couple spotted the police vehicle parked in front of a wrecked automobile. As they slowed down, an officer with a flashlight waved them on.

CHAPTER 47

WHEN THE COUPLE ARRIVED IN DALLAS, THEY parked downtown. After talking for a while, they hugged and kissed goodbye, and Sabine caught a cab to the airport. The minute she embarked, she immediately grabbed a pillow and blanket before sitting down in first class. The flight attendant offered her some champagne, she declined. Sabine was tired; her day had started at two a.m. As the plane began to taxi, she took off her shoes, covered herself with her blanket, laid her head against her pillow, closed her eyes, and woke up eight hours later.

Rich experienced emptiness and loss after Sabine left him at the car rental agency, and he felt sad when her cab drove away. The couple had been through hell the past few weeks, and the dangers they had faced as a team had reinforced the love and respect they had for each other. At the last minute, and for security's sake, Rich made a few more changes regarding his coming travel. In the afternoon, he would fly out to Germany and call Sabine after landing in Frankfurt to give her the time of his arrival at the Gare de l'Est train station in Paris. He would travel from Germany to France by train. Rich turned in his vehicle then caught a taxi to the Dallas airport. It would be a long day until he boarded his flight at four p.m.

Once on the plane, the agent desired only one thing, sleep. Rich was still exhausted when he came out of customs in Frankfurt almost ten hours later. To kill time, he caught a taxi to downtown Frankfurt and decided to spend some time in a museum where there would be minimal noise and traffic. After lunch, it was time to get back to the airport to fetch his backpack from the left-luggage locker and go to the train station. He was surprised to find out that a train leaves Frankfurt to Paris every fifty-nine minutes, and the ride takes six hours or less. His would-be short, only four hours and at a very reasonable price of forty-nine euros. As his train left Frankfurt, he wasted no time contacting Sabine to give her his arrival time. Wanting to make sure no one was tracking his calls, the conversation was brief.

Rich tried to rest. For some reason, he became sullen, jumpy at times, with feelings of being watched. Arriving in Paris, the agent regained his composure, felt robust, relaxed, and wide awake. Due to a large crowd on the platform, he did not immediately spot Sabine, who was waiting at the end of platform four. As usual, she was dressed in clothes that flattered her body, nothing fancy, her light gray tee-shirt, some ankle tights, and her eternal trench coat.

They felt alone in the middle of the densely packed crowd. Nothing could keep Rich and Sabine from embracing as if they had been separated a full year. Finally, hand in hand, the couple walked out of the train station.

As they walked toward Sabine's car, an older couple walked toward them. With a big smile, the man brought his right hand to his forehead in a salute. Rich saluted Colonel Andy. The agent and his partner, who had been kept in the dark, were taken aback to see Marguerite and Andy together. Apparently, Andy had been successful in winning back Marguerite's heart. Sabine had called her mother as soon as she landed in Paris, but Marguerite never mentioned Andy was part of her life again; she wanted to surprise both Rich and Sabine, and she did. Marguerite invited Sabine and Rich to a get-together the next day.

As the two couples hugged, Andy whispered in Rich's ear. "Our French friend, Captain Victor Coutare, has left a gift for you in the car. Make sure you keep it on you." The agent was expecting the gun Andy was referring to. Rich asked, "Have you heard anything from POTUS?"

"Not yet, but my gut or instinct tells me something is about to take place."

As the group walked toward their car, a man about six feet tall, wearing a navy blue suit, watched the two couples walking away from the train station. Around his kneck was a white clerical collar worn by priests.

CHAPTER 48

T HE FOLLOWING FIVE DAYS WERE SOMEWHAT HECTIC due to a big event being planned; Andy and Marguerite's civil marriage ceremony. Sabine and Rich had made reservations to take the couple on a sightseeing cruise to celebrate their special day. After a detour to the local city hall where Andy and Marguerite would be officially married, a gourmet lunch would be served on the boat.

Saturday was a bright, promising sunny day. Keeping all the festivities and the number of guests to a minimum allowed everybody to relax and be cheerful. Marguerite was wearing a demure pale gray suit and a pair of sexy d'Orsay pumps that matched an adorable bridal purse. At the town hall, the mayor made a short speech, delivered the marriage certificate, shook hands, and offered his best wishes to the couple. Sabine took a few pictures, and the four of them walked to the boat where the mini reception was to take place. Aware of the special event, the cruise management had brightened up the guests' table with a beautiful flower arrangement made of white orchids, fragrant Asian lilies, and delicate gypsophila.

At the dining room entrance, po-faced Sabine said, "Rich, do you remember the last time we were here?" Feeling sheepish at first, Rich regained his composure. He said, "Yes, I do, and I have regretted acting so distant and maybe even rude that day, but remember, I did not know you well then, we had just met, so I did not think I needed to inform you I was leaving."

Sabine took a few more pictures of the dining room, especially of the table decorated and set with style and refinement. The lunch was one to be remembered. It started with champagne, courtesy of the restaurant, accompanied by caviar and creme fraiche tartlets. The rest of the feast was delicious and met Sabine and Rich's expectations.

They were ending their meal with coffee and dessert when Rich said he had to make an announcement. At that precise moment, a waiter appeared with a bottle of fifty-year brandy that he served in crystal after dinner glasses. Rich never verbally announced anything. Instead, he pulled a velvet-covered box out of his pocket, lifted the lid, faced Sabine, and said, "Sabine, will you marry me?"

Surprised and emotional, Sabine could not control her voice; she was at a loss for words. Finally, she got up to hug Rich and uttered a loud 'yes.' Rich slid a single diamond engagement ring on Sabine's finger. Andy and Marguerite were as surprised and happy as their daughter. The four continued their journey, passing several structures of historical importance, such as the Eiffel Tower and the Louvre Museum.

The newlyweds went home to prepare their luggage and get ready to fly to the Spanish island of Mallorca. Rich and his fiancee would stay in Marguerite's cozy apartment after they dropped the newlyweds off at the airport.

Rich and Sabine dropped Andy and Marguerite off in front of terminal 2F to catch the Airbus A319, flight AF 1658 to Palma de Mallorca at six p.m. In the vast terminal, just a few feet away, was an individual dressed in a dark suit with a white clerical collar, one of the Brothers of Saint Longinus who had been following Sabine and Rich earlier. Little did the couple know that somehow this same priest would follow them again as they left the airport.

CHAPTER 49

Rich and Sabine held hands as the silver Airbus sped down the runway for take-off. Once the aircraft was out of site, Rich turned toward Sabine, "We need to head for their car. Andy left an envelope for me under the spare tire."

"Do you know what's in it?" Sabine quickly replied as her pupils enlarged.

"Not exactly. But I believe Andy wants me to go after Henri Dubois, the head of security who works exclusively at the Rothchild's holiday home on the French Riviera and accompanies family members when traveling. He is often present on the Rothchilds' yacht when festivities take place on the luxury watercraft. Rich studied Sabine, waiting for a reaction, then continued. "I can't wait to see what is in that package."

Sabine slid her left hand into Rich's right hand and squeezed. "You will probably need help. I hope you are not planning on trying to take on that scum by yourself."

Rich did not want to put Sabine in harm's way, but he would need her eyes and ears. "This job will be different, maybe more complicated than before, simply because civilians will surround Dubois, and for that reason, I will need you." As he opened the trunk, Rich l kissed her on the cheek. Giggling, she said, "I will do it, but because we are now officially engaged, you have to stop taking unnecessary chances."

Rich reached under the spare tire and pulled out the sealed envelope. The temptation was great to open it right then, even though he knew it was safer to do that once in Marguerite's comfortable and secured home. The information inside the envelope could not be exposed. It originated from an intercepted memo sent by Dubois to an unknown recipient. Any revelation of the contents could result in diplomatic repercussions.

As Rich and Sabine pulled out of the airport parking lot in their small Peugeot, another vehicle, a Renault with a priest driving, followed the couple.

As they drove along, Rich spotted the patisserie (pastry shop) that Sabine had recommended to him numerous times, so to be the judge of the products sold there, he stopped for coffee and to try one of the mouthwatering pastries. After parking, Rich could no longer wait to find out what the orders inside the large envelope were. The couple entered the shop and ordered two Napoleons, those flaky pastries filled with a thick crème patissière, a creamy custard.

After a few sips of coffee, a bit anxious, Rich nervously opened the envelope and smiled as he read the first word on the top sheet, 'son.' He knew that Andy had always considered him and treated him as the son he never had. After reading the personal information, he turned to Sabine and read the operation information compiled by Andy. 'The Rothchild's one hundred and forty-seven-foot yacht will be docked for the next two weeks in the port of Hercule, in the Monaco natural bay at the foot of the ancestral rock of the princes of Monaco. The Saudi Arabia third prince in line to the throne will also be there with his two-hundred thirty seven foot yacht. The prince and the Rothchilds' representant will meet to discuss a proposal for Natural Gas to be shipped to France. Due to the prince's visit, security will be almost equal to that provided to the United States president.' The introduction was followed with details about where precisely the yachts would be docked in the port.

Rich laid the document down, took a bite of his pastry, then a long sip of coffee, and continued reading Andy's message. 'My French friend, Victor Coutaire, will supply all the arms and intelligence you will need. He will also provide escape help for you should you be in a bind. Because he is a retired military officer, he prefers not to be involved in terminating anyone on French soil.' Sabine interrupted with a valid question, "Will the Rothchilds' representant and the prince be meeting on land?"

"No." Rich took another bite and sip of coffee, and then he resumed reading Andy's message. 'Victor will provide explosives and other devices you might need. You are to give him twenty-four to forty-eight hours to deliver after you contact him with your shopping list.' Having shared all the information with Sabine, Rich said, "Do you still feel up to another challenge?" Deep down in his heart, the agent was hoping Sabine would say no, but his expectation cut short when she answered,

"I want to participate in the elimination of those creepy individuals who work for the Rothchilds. I won't miss the opportunity to protect you." The protection Sabine mentioned amused Rich, who could not help giggling.

"I knew you would say that, but let it be known, it is going to be complicated and dangerous, this is going to be a naval operation. Now, let's prepare a list of arms we must have; we can't waste any time.

If Andy's friend can get what I want, we should be able to leave for Monaco within a couple of days."

Sabine ordered more coffee, and Rich began to write down the list of necessary weapons. To make it easier for Victor, the agent decided to order French arms that Victor had used in his career. They would not only be readily available; they would also be some of the best made in the world.

CHAPTER 50

A s Sabine set the coffee on the table, she said, "You look pensive, what's on your mind?"

Rich furtively looked around to make sure no one could hear, then said, "I've decided to go with French-made arms. I will read off what I came up with, and if you can think of anything else, tell me."

"Where did Andy meet Victor?"

"Victor was on special patrol in Afghanistan. ISIS pinned him and his men down. Though outnumbered, Andy and his squad somehow worked their way under fire and brought out to safely the ambushed Captain Coutaire and his men. This courageous and selfless intervention on Andy's initiative moved Victor. As a result, the French captain never forgot the brave gesture that saved him and his men. As a result, Victor considers Andy his brother-in-arms and would give his life to help him."

"Now, you understand why a Frenchman is helping our cause."

Rich began to go over the list. "Two Glock 17's with silencers and ten mags. Two HK MP & fold up Submachine guns. The ones that us 4.6 x 30mm ammo, and of course, silencers. One PGM Ultima Ratio 7.62 mm sniper rifle with a silencer." Rich laid his paper on the table and looked at Sabine.

"You better ask for some C4 just in case we have to open a door or two."

"Good idea. I am sure our target has bulletproof rooms on board. I will ask Victor for four blocks of C4, detonation mechanisms, and timers. Anything else?"

"Do you still have your seal knife?"

"Yes, and I would not leave home without it. I will order one more." The couple then changed the subject and began to talk about how they would get to Monaco. Would it be a direct one hour and thirty-minute flight, a six-hour train ride with a change in Nice, twenty-five miles from Monaco, or a nine to ten-hour car journey? It was decided, they would take a TGV (high-speed train) to get there.

"Before I forget, Andy mentioned that two additional men would attend the meeting in Monaco, Retired Lt. General Richard C. Clarkston and retired Major General Theodore R. Williams. They are figureheads for the arms sales corporations. His note also informs that they are now top members of the Bilderberger group and top strategists for The CCC."

Sabine did not hesitate to put her two-cents worth. "The more, the merrier. I am ready for them. Three vermins will be eliminated."

Once they finished their coffee, Rich took out his cell phone and dialed the number to contact Victor. On the fourth ring, Rich heard a hello in French but no introduction. Rich gave the code words found in the envelope and then waited.

The person on the line instructed Rich to meet Victor at the Eiffel tower's bottom stairs in two hours. The couple left and drove to a parking lot not far from their destination and walked to the meeting place. Incognito, a priest was following them.

It was time to meet Victor. They were now a few feet away from the tower's bottom stairs. Ten minutes had passed, Sabine and Rich began to worry. Another ten minutes slowly dragged. Finally, a short man about five foot seven, smoking a cigarette, approached them. A code word was given, but no greeting or introduction followed. Victor looked around and asked for the list Rich had prepared. Smoke passed through Victor's nostrils as he read the list. Raising his head, he said, "I will have your supplies. Your package will be in Nice the day after tomorrow at the train station. Here is a key to locker 1726. Be cautious inside the station, and as you leave the station, there are cameras everywhere."

Rich offered to pay Victor, but he became upset and said, "I owe your colonel a big favor. By the way, do you have a guard, a priest protecting you? Both Sabine and Rich were lost for words; they stared at Victor with puzzled looks. Victor realized the couple was unaware of their stalker. "I was here when you were standing by the tower, wondering if I would show up. I observed this priest watching you. I noticed he was moving in synchrony with you." Rich said, "I bet the Vatican has sent a member of The Brothers Of Saint Longinus to eliminate us."

"Let me reassure you. Andy asked me to watch over you. The priest will no longer stalk you because he is dead, on his way to purgatory. Victor gave a half-suppressed laugh and added, I used my friend, the garrote, to send him to hell. Like him, I have been following you from the airport to that pastry shop. You did not see him, but he was there. If you don't need anything else, I'll go now." The couple was stunned by Victor's surprising revelation. Rich came out of his silence to thank Victor Coutaire.

"We don't know how to thank you, but if you ever need us, we have your back."

Victor bowed, took a long drag on his cigarette, shook hands with Sabine and Rich, and left. Sabine suggested they rest after all these developments that could have been tragic. "Let's go to my mother's place to relax before we start packing and get on the road."

CHAPTER 51

THE FOLLOWING MORNING, AFTER PACKING, RICH consulted the train schedule. Ten Paris to Nice trains, five of the high speed, were available throughout the day. Rich said, "When you are ready, I want you to take a cab to the Gare de Lyon train station and get a first-class ticket for yourself. After you leave the apartment, I will do the same thing, go to the same station and purchase a second class ticket on the same train. We will stay apart for the six hours it will take to get to Nice, and if you should bump into me in the snack bar, we will ignore each other." Sabine did not think this excessive vigilance was called for, but of course, she would comply. She had noticed that Rich looked upset, "What concerns you now? Victor took care of one of our nemeses. You should rejoice."

"Yes, he did, but we don't know who else the CCC has hired to take his place. I wonder what he did with the priest's body." Almost laughing, he added, "It could be rotting at the bottom of the Eiffel Tower. Let's not take any chances."

As they were finishing packing, Sabine addressed Rich, "Earlier, you were giving me some speculative information about President Kennedy, and you were going to tell me something else before we got interrupted. Do you remember what you were about to say to me?"

Rich scratched his neck as he usually did when trying to remember something, a sort of tic. "Yes, now, I remember. I told you that many believe the CIA and Vice President Johnson were involved in Kennedy's assassination. The CCC wanted this war in Vietnam as there was a lot of money to be made. President Kennedy was not going along with the idea. The CCC knew the Texan Vice President would jump on board to increase his wealth. Shortly after a meeting with the heads of state in Texas, the President was dead. Test after test proved that one sniper couldn't use the recovered gun to shoot as fast as he did to kill Kennedy. There was also one possible witness who was also conveniently shot. As you may know, this country's youth rebelled following this tragic and violent incident, and Johnson never ran for reelection. The war-making machine of the US is lucrative, brings in loads of money for the CCC."

"Was the issue that took place in Iran with Carter planned?"

"Carter was one of the few honest Presidents that we ever had. The CCC set him up by causing gas shortages and severe inflation in the country. He never had a chance for a second term.

It was time for Sabine to leave her mother's apartment, catch a taxi cab, and get on the train to Nice. Rich surprised her when he said, "If I am not where we are to meet within twenty-four hours, you return to Paris." She insisted they leave Paris together, but Rich had made up his mind to adhere to his original plans.

"I will be there. Now, go." They hugged then kissed goodbye. Rich watched the street until the taxi was out of sight.

The agent chambered a round in the gun that the colonel had given him at the airport. He secured the apartment, locked the door, and kept the key he would return to Sabine later. Before leaving, he put on a disguise.

Once on the train, Rich took out the folded brown envelope and went over the information again. Rich had noted that, after the elimination of Pierre Paquet, the Paris new head of security for the Rothchild family was Herman Walker, a former British special forces (SAS) captain. Rich was aware of the SAS operatives; they were considered equal to, or sometimes above the Navy Seals. Rich did not think he would be dealing with this skilled and dangerous individual on the Riviera.

As the TGV whisked along the track, it was hard to distinguish some of the signs and sites. The train was going over two hundred kilometers an hour at times. In the rail passenger service domain, Japan and Europe are light years ahead of the United States, which may not be valid for freight shipments.

Rich turned to the next page to continue reading about the current assignment. 'You can expect to see Richard C. Clarkston and Theodore R. Williams, former Army Generals, at the meeting. They have been responsible for cost overruns in military arms production and selling non-listed approved military armory to the Saudis. They must be eliminated if at all possible. The report switched to another contemptible individual.

STOP: The Saudi prince Mohammed bin Ahmed III was linked to the 9/11 incidence. The prince, guarded at all times by former high trained US military personnel. STOP: They will be staying on their yacht in the bay of Monaco. STOP: If safe, it might be best to take them down on their craft. Have two escape routes planned? Monaco will shut the area down as soon as the incident is reported. STOP: Do not take chances. Son, you and my daughter, are worth more to me than any sacrifice designed to clean up the mess this country is faced with, not even in the name of democracy. STOP.

CHAPTER 52

The couple had breakfast at different locations before meeting at the pier, where almost all the small fishing boats had left out to sea.

Five hundred euros rented the partners an eighteen-foot fishing boat for five hours. As the couple passed the Rothchild's big yacht's bow, port side, stern, and starboard, Sabine took numerous pictures with Rich's iPhone. Once out past the craft, they studied the pictures. From a non-suspicious distance, they watched the yacht with binoculars to see the surveillance pattern that the guards used to patrol the deck. Moving around the craft, they tried to find ways to get on board during the night's darkness. As they were ready to return toward shore, Rich smiled when he saw what he had been looking for; the tie lines hanging down from the vessel's port side.

Back on land, they perused the photos in search of options to get on board the craft. Sitting on the warm sand, Rich estimated the yacht's distance from shore and other boats berthed in the bay.

He looked at Sabine and said, "Let's go find an out of the way restaurant for lunch. I have an idea I think we should consider."

A few miles from the casino, on Avenue De L'Annonciade, near the Chemin De La Rousse, they found a secluded cafe. While they ate a riviera specialty called a bouillabaisse, a rich and spicy soup made with various local fish and seashells, Rich shared his plan.

"Sabine, have you ever done any scuba diving?"

"No. But I have watched many Jacques Cousteau documentaries. It should not be too hard. Why?"

"We are going to rent some scuba gear. I can teach you the basics in a couple of hours, enough for what we are going to do." Rich finished the food on his plate, and the waiter took their order for dessert and coffee. The agent said, "I am going to rent the gear and buy a small rubber raft that will take us to the yacht. We will use an electric motor for power." The server appeared with the apricot tartlets and coffee.

Rich took a bite of his pie, then a long sip of coffee. "In the darkness, we should be able to get close to the yacht without being seen. I will tie our scuba gear on a rope and hang it just under the water on the ship's aft. After I sink the rubber raft, it will be time to go aboard the yacht to eliminate as many of those vermins as possible. If I cannot get into the prince's room, I will plant C4 with a timer. As soon as we complete our assignment, we jump overboard."

"How do I get the gear on underwater?"

"Put the mouthpiece in your mouth and turn the valve on the tank to the left. That is all there is to it. I will help you get the pack on, and for safety, I will tie a rope from you to me, so you don't get lost, something similar to a leash." Rich could not help laughing while Sabine appeared perturbed. He resumed, "I guess this sounds like an Indiana

Jones adventure to you. We will go over everything as soon as I rent the gear."

Something kept bothering Rich, the gear's disposal, but most of all, Sabine's safety, which was always foremost in his mind. Then it dawned on him; he remembered a device he had used in the army on several occasions to get close to boats and back onshore without a trail of telltale bubbles appearing underwater. A rebreather was the answer. Though they were a little more dangerous than regular scuba tanks, the apparatus could stay underwater up to six hours, depending on the unit's size. After mentioning the device to Sabine, she quickly asked what it was.

"A rebreather is a breathing device that partially purifies the exhaled breath by removing some of the carbon dioxide and mixing the air left with oxygen to be breathed again by the diver. The unit also allows you to stay down much longer, and with it, there is almost no worry about decompression."

"Is it more difficult to use?"

"Not at all. My worry is, can we find one here?"

"There are several scuba and sports shops."

"I saw them too. Listen, this is important. Please, go back to the casino while I go try to locate and rent the rebreathers and see about getting wet suits. Those idle people we saw last night at the casino, they spend half their time drinking. You may encounter some of the guests we are after. If you do, try to accost them, and if needed, pretend you are soliciting, short of offering services. You may find out information essential to us, like when they will be leaving Monaco.

Rich finished drinking his coffee, and after sitting his cup down, he said, "Let's do it. We will meet in your room at eight p.m. It should be dark by then."

The couple left the cafe together and separated at the door.

CHAPTER 53

As the train pulled into Monaco, the sun was setting behind the blue waters of the Mediterranean. The gold and orange colors were so vibrant that Rich could only stare at the beauty mother nature offered to all. As something touched him, his right hand, with lightning speed, slid under his left arm, reaching for his gun. Then he heard, "Rich, love, it's me, Sabine, relax."

Sabine could hear the sigh of relief as Rich turned. The hard cold face of someone trained to kill changed to that of one in love. "Hon, cough, or say something, my love before you approach from behind." Then he took Sabine's small carry on by the handle, through his pack over his shoulder, and said, "Let's find two small hotels close to the Casino de Monte Carlo.

You register in one, and I will stay in the other. Let's try not to be seen together. I will go back inside the train station and get the package Victor has waiting for us."

After returning with the package, the couple walked toward the hotels. While Sabine signed in at one hotel, Rich went around the block and signed in at another, still wearing his disguise. Both had agreed to shower and go to the casino at nine pm.

It was a few minutes after eight-forty pm when Rich walked into the casino. He found himself in a completely different world. It was a glittering venue filled by rich people and beautiful women. The atrium seemed to reach the stars above his head. The artwork on the walls and the sculptures set among fountains would be worth millions. The gaming tables, leather-bound and hand-carved, made Las Vegas tables look like something bought at Walmart.

Being mesmerized, he never heard a cocktail waitress walk up to him.

She was dressed and attractive enough to be an L.A. actress. After taking a full champagne glass and an appetizer, he searched for those he had come to eliminate. It did not take long; Paquet was next to a sheik, obviously one of the Saud prince's. There were two more guards not far away. Rich could see the bulge of guns beneath there suit jackets.

As he studied the group, he soon spotted another woman, one more beautiful inside and out, above all the others. Sabine had entered the casino wearing a flattering semi-long black chiffon dress. She touched her right ear to acknowledge that she had spotted Rich.

Separately the two mingled with the crowd, taking note of the security guards, the cameras, and the exits. Suddenly, Rich almost choked on his appetizer; at the roulette table, two men he was not expecting to see here: The two Generals, Mr. Richard C. Clarkston and Mr. Theodore R. Williams, both top members of The CCC. Richard worked his way toward Sabine; once he was close enough, he whispered to her to watch the two CCC members and see where they go.

It was after one am when Rich saw Sabine leave behind the two CCC members. Rich continued to watch his prey Henri Dubois and the Saudi prince. Suddenly, Rich saw Henri, the Rothschilds' security top dog. They're all here under one roof, he thought. Rich continued to watch the group and was astonished by the massive amounts of dollars that the prince was losing at the gambling table. As the hours passed, fatigue set in, but he had to find out which boat anchored in Port Hercules the group was staying. Being the only deep-water port in Monaco, Rich was glad he did not have to look elsewhere for his prey.

It was three thirty-five am when the CCC members, the prince, and the three guards left the casino. Staying in the shadows, Rich followed the group to the water's edge. It was not long before they got into a deluxe tender and sped toward the yachts anchored in the bay. Rich could guess which vessel they were staying, the longest one, almost two hundred feet long. Having the information he wanted, Rich left and worked his way back toward Sabine's hotel. Soon he caught up with a short petite woman who was going in the same direction. It was Sabine. Few words were exchanged as they stepped back into the shadows, then Sabine said, "Your two CCC members got on a small boat that took them out to that big yacht in the bay. What did you find out?"

"Same thing. It's good; you know that group are all staying in the same place." I don't see any way we can take them down in the casino and getaway. Since the assault will take place on the yacht, we need to rent a fishing boat and recon the yacht. When we attack, once onboard, we'll neutralize the guards and then take care of the CCC members, the prince who was behind 9/11 and that killer, Paquet."

"I'm exhausted, Rich. Could you sneak up to my place and tuck me in?"

Then a sensual smile appeared on Sabine's face.

"As tired as I am, I would move heaven and earth to tuck you in bed. What floor and room are you in?"

"I made sure I was on the first floor. I am in the back, the first window from the back right corner of the hotel." After kissing Rich, Sabine headed for her hotel, and sneaking behind her in the shadows was Rich.

A man in disguise began to crawl through the window that Sabine had opened.

Once inside the couple shared a long shower that inevitably triggered some amorous feelings. After they dried each other off, they collapsed in bed.

Sabine did not remember what time Rich slipped out through the window and returned to his hotel.

CHAPTER 54

THE COUPLE HAD BREAKFAST AT DIFFERENT LOCATIONS before meeting at the pier, where almost all the small fishing boats had left out to sea.

Five hundred euros rented the partners an eighteen-foot fishing boat for five hours. As the couple passed the Rothchild's big yacht's bow, port side, stern, and starboard, Sabine took numerous pictures with Rich's iPhone. Once out past the craft, they studied the pictures. From a non-suspicious distance, they watched the yacht with binoculars to see the surveillance pattern that the guards used to patrol the deck. Moving around the craft, they tried to find ways to get on board during the night's darkness. As they were ready to return toward shore, Rich smiled when he saw what he had been looking for; the tie lines hanging down from the vessel's port side.

Back on land, they perused the photos in search of options to get on board the craft. Sitting on the warm sand, Rich estimated the yacht's distance from both shore and other boats berthed in the bay.

He looked at Sabine and said, "Let's go find an out of the way restaurant for lunch. I have an idea I think we should consider."

A few miles from the casino, on Avenue De L'Annonciade, near the Chemin De La Rousse, they found a secluded cafe. While they ate a riviera specialty called a bouillabaisse, a rich and spicy soup made with various local fish and seashells, Rich shared his plan.

"Sabine, have you ever done any scuba diving?"

"No. But I have watched many Jacques Cousteau documentaries. It should not be too hard. Why?"

"We are going to rent some scuba gear. I can teach you the basics in a couple of hours, enough for what we are going to do." Rich finished the food on his plate, and the waiter took their order for dessert and coffee. The agent said, "I am going to rent the gear and buy a small rubber raft that will take us to the yacht. We will use an electric motor for power." The server appeared with the apricot tartlets and coffee.

Rich took a bite of his pie, then a long sip of coffee. "In the darkness, we should be able to get close to the yacht without being seen. I will tie our scuba gear on a rope and hang it just under the water on the ship's aft. After I sink the rubber raft, it will be time to go aboard the yacht to eliminate as many of those vermins as possible. If I cannot get into the prince's room, I will plant C4 with a timer. As soon as we complete our assignment, we jump overboard."

"How do I get the gear on underwater?"

"Put the mouthpiece in your mouth and turn the valve on the tank to the left. That is all there is to it. I will help you get the pack on, and for safety, I will tie a rope from you to me, so you don't get lost, something similar to a leash." Rich could not help laughing while Sabine appeared perturbed. He resumed, "I guess this sounds like an Indiana

Jones adventure to you. We will go over everything as soon as I rent the gear."

Something kept bothering Rich, the gear's disposal, but most of all, Sabine's safety, which was always foremost in his mind. Then it dawned on him; he remembered a device he had used in the army on several occasions to get close to boats and back onshore without a trail of telltale bubbles appearing underwater. A rebreather was the answer. Though they were a little more dangerous than regular scuba tanks, the apparatus could stay underwater up to six hours, depending on the unit's size. After mentioning the device to Sabine, she quickly asked what it was.

"A rebreather is a breathing device that partially purifies the exhaled breath by removing some of the carbon dioxide and mixing the air left with oxygen to be breathed again by the diver. The unit also allows you to stay down much longer, and with it, there is almost no worry about decompression."

"Is it more difficult to use?"

"Not at all. My worry is, can we find one here?"

"There are several scuba and sports shops."

"I saw them too. Listen, this is important. Please, go back to the casino while I try to locate and rent the rebreathers and see about getting wet suits. Those idle people we saw last night at the casino, they spend half their time drinking. You may encounter some of the guests we are after. If you do, try to accost them, and if needed, pretend you are soliciting, short of offering services. You may find out information essential to us, like when they will be leaving Monaco.

Rich finished drinking his coffee, and after sitting his cup down, he said, "Let's do it. We will meet in your room at eight p.m. It should be dark by then."

The couple left the cafe together and separated at the door.

CHAPTER 55

RICH WAS GETTING FRUSTRATED AFTER LEAVING THE three diving shop. None of the stores carried rebreathers, and none offered to locate the apparatus for him except the last store, but with no definite promise of delivery. Time was of the essence. Rich did not know how long the CCC members would sojourn in Monaco. He had no idea when the entire gang would be sailing away.

Rich kicked a few small pebbles off the sidewalk as he walked toward Sabine's hotel. After two quick taps on her window, the drapes pulled back. Knowing her man would be there any minute, Sabine had changed into the only sexy loungewear she had brought with her. Pearl in color, with a low neckline loose camisole, this little outfit was very feminine. She shouted, "Hello, handsome. You came to save a damsel in distress and carry her off to love her forever."

Rich's muscular body slid through the window without grace. He could hardly keep from laughing. Once inside, he said, "Never in my life have I laughed like I do with you. Now, do you want the bad news?"

"Before you announce the bad news, I think you should rest and maybe relax under a hot shower."

"You keep that up, and I will forget what I have to say. Curiously, there are no rebreathers available in this resort by the sea. One dealer offered to order them for me, but he did not know how long it would take to deliver. He was vague, and I don't want to take a chance, not knowing how long our organized group of criminals will be staying here." To amuse Rich, Sabine shared how the two generals had approached her in the casino. As Rich had predicted, they were at one of the bars, drinking whiskey. "Because I was alone, paying attention to my surroundings, they thought I was a hooker looking for johns. I didn't contradict them, on the contrary. The head of security offered me a trip to Marseille. The two old Generals suggested getting in my pants in exchange for a generous financial reward and a gourmet dinner at the famous 3 Michelin star restaurant called Le Louis XV Alain Ducasse. Lacking finesse, those two crude characters bragged about the extravagant price of the meal." Sabine laughed and said, "It is my turn to deliver bad news. The whole group is sailing out tonight except for General Clarkston, who is flying back to Paris later today. I heard them say he would be back in Marseille late tomorrow."

"How far is Marseille from here?"

"I looked it up, just over 221 kilometers. According to the guard, the yacht is leaving at ten p.m. Everyone is going except Clarkston."

Rich was not familiar with this big city. "I have never been to Marseille. Whats is it like?"

"It's a crossroads for immigration and trade since the Greeks in six-hundred BC. At its heart is the Vieux-Port (Old Harbor), where fishmongers sell their catch along the boat-lined quay. The harbor is deep, and even cruise ships can dock there."

"Did you, by chance, hear how long they might be staying?"

"They all thought they would stay close to a week. The prince wanted to visit the Basilique Notre-Dame-de-la-Garde, a Romanesque-Byzantine church. I heard one of the guards mention things that made no sense to me. He talked about Corbusier's influential Cité Radieuse complex and Zaha Hadid's CMA CGM Tower. I recorded all that I heard. Oh, I also overheard the same guard say they were not to forget to deliver the package. Those were his words. That's pretty much everything."

"You never told me how you got rid of the generals." Rich started laughing as Sabine pushed him on his back and straddled him. Suddenly Rich became very quiet and even gloomy. Having Sabine around had transformed his life. Not only was she warm, kind, and loyal, but she was also open and sincere, two qualities that had been lacking from most of the people he had encountered during his lifetime. With sorrowful eyes, the agent started talking.

"I never had a life before I met you. It's nice to be able to relax, love, be loved, and be myself." Sabine to reply, "You are finally learning how to live at my contact. This state of mind is called 'joie de vivre,' meaning keen enjoyment of living. You can experience this feeling of great happiness only when you keep your life simple. To remain relatively free of stress, one must do most everything slowly, not fast,

fast, fast. This 'joie de vivre' is not dependent upon one's success or financial status. It is present when one adopts a laid-back attitude on life. Appreciate what you have. Too much ambition and envy often bring the opposite to 'joie de vivre,' which is dispiritedness and disconnection."

After listening to Sabine's speech and learning the bad news, the yacht's imminent departure, Rich decided that he and Sabine they would leave Monaco right away and go by train to Marseille. As for the rebreathers, Rich elected to contact Captain Victor Coutaire. "This guy should be able to get rebreathers for us. After all, he located all the arms we wanted." Sabine suggested Rich ask Victor to bring the devices to them. "He sounds like someone who is missing the action the military offers. I am sure that we can use his expertise."

"That may be a good idea. I will call Coutaire while we are on the train. Now, get packed and catch a taxi cab to the train station; I will be right behind you with the precious duffel bag full of goodies. Again, we take separate seats on the train." At the train station, the couple spotted each other but acted like strangers.

CHAPTER 56

A s the train sped toward Marseille, all Rich could hear was the monotonous clap, clap, clap of the metal wheels pounding on the railway tracks. He had asked for and got a seat on the train's seaside from which he stared at the Mediterranean's blue waters. Alone, the agent had time to contemplate how to approach Victor to convince him to join him and Sabine. He knew the ex-legionnaire could be an asset in their fight against the CCC.

Rich removed his iPhone from his backpack and pushed the speed button connecting him with Victor. A deep and rough smoker's voice answered the phone on the second ring. The agent returned the greeting and gave the code word as there was always the possibility someone was monitoring the call. "Captain Coutaire, I need your help."

"No problem. Be careful what you say."

"You remember the op you went on with Andy off Iran?"

"Of course I do."

"I need two of those square things, the instruments you used so not to be seen going in and leaving."

The intentional vagueness to describe the articles in question led Coutaire to remain quiet for several seconds to think. "Ah! Now, I remember. If we are talking about the same thing, and I know we are, that's no problem; I can get this in a few days."

"I don't have a few days." I am arriving in the French city known for the white stuff in less than two hours. What can you do for me?" Victor figured Rich was on his way to Marseille, a city known by everyone as the drug's entry in Europe.

"I will call you in one hour with my flight number. I will expect you at the airport. You can count on me." Rich needed help from Victor, but he did not want this man to endanger his life.

"This operation could be difficult, and I do not wish to get you directly involved."

"Getting involved would help me repay Andy for his selfless commitment toward me." There were numerous dry coughs. "I repeat, you can count on me if you change your mind. I will call you soon." Then the phone went dead.

Rich did not know what to do; he was worried about Andy's friend getting hurt, but he also knew that he was well trained as an ex-legionnaire and could get aboard the yacht quietly, exterminate, and disappear. So much was going on; he was not aware of the time until his phone vibrated against an hour later.

"I leave 20:30, arrive at 21:45 on Air France, AF7728. No problem with the items you need. I am glad I can be of service.

CHAPTER 57

ANOTHER HOUR HAD PASSED. THE TRAIN WAS NOW entering the huge Marseille-Saint-Charles train station. The structure built in 1848 was linked to the city by a magnificent staircase that left the couple speechless. Rich signaled to Sabine to follow him at a distance. Soon they met in the shadows of the train station, and after a badly needed hug, Rich shared with his partner what had transpired on the train.

"We need to rent a room out of the way, close to the dock. "Get Marseille on your phone and find us a map of the city. Sabine searched for information about the city for a few minutes, then said, "To stay close to the dock, we will have to take separate taxis to the Ferry terminal. Once there, we will catch another cab and go to the Rue Vacon, where there are many small hotels. This street is served by buses to the city every ten minutes."

An hour had passed before the couple settled into their lodging. When Rich looked at his watch, he noted he had less than an hour to get to the airport. "I am on my way to meet Victor. Because we should not be seen together at the airport, you stay here."

"Rich, listen to me. I know Victor. No one will suspect me if I pick him up. While I do that, you take care of the car. We will meet you at the car rental.

Rich hesitated at first, but Sabine stood steadfast. He respected her common sense and finally gave in. The couple caught separate cabs to the Marseille Provence Airport. Sabine stood by the arrival exit for just over twenty minutes before spotting Captain Victor Coutaire walk toward her. Victor waved his hand flat across in front of him, signaling he would follow Sabine. Since the traveler had his backpack hanging over his left shoulder, there was no luggage to pick up.

The couple walked separately down the aisles and toward the car rental agencies. It was not long before Rich came out of the shadows and said, "Good to see you. Follow me to my rented Peugeot." Rich started to get in the car when Victor stepped up and said, "Why don't you give me the keys? Driving in Marseille is not simple, and it is even worse as you get close to the docks. I used to live here; in fact, I received my underwater training in Marseille."

The conversation was delivered in broken English, but the partners understood the message. During the ride, Rich shared with Victor what he had planned to achieve in Monaco, but never did. After the trio moved through the traffic to reach the Vieux Port, Victor made a right turn and drove down the Q du Port road toward Fort St Jean. All of a sudden, he slowed down and pulled off to the side of the road. I know it is getting dark but look just up ahead. You can see yachts, and the one belonging to your friends is called Muhammad bin Salman. It is berthed here where the water is deep." Victor lit up his second Gitane cigarette since leaving the airport. "Now, we go a little farther. I want to show you something else."

It was not long before they were on the grounds of the Fort Saint-Jean Historic waterfront military structure. Victor drove to the edge of the water and said, "From here, your sniper has only a four hundred plus meter shot onto the yacht. Who is your sniper?"

There was a long silence, then Rich replied, "Sabine is my sniper." Rich was waiting to get a reaction from the captain, maybe even an objection, Sabine being a female. At that moment, the agent realised that Coutaire did not know what role Sabine played in this operation. Was she a troop follower, a girlfriend, a wife, or a genuine agent? Rich added, "She has seconded me on several assignments, and makes shots that I would have a difficult time making. Besides, I want her in a safe place to exit from when the shit hits the fan."

"If you have binoculars, bring them out, and let's take a short walk."

Close to the water's edge, Victor showed the couple an excellent spot for Sabine to hide and still have good scope coverage of the yacht's top deck. Addressing Sabine, he said," Once your assignment is over, wipe off your rifle and throw it in the sea. The water is extremely deep here, and make sure you leave nothing behind. Then walk back to the vehicle, which will be parked in a different spot. I will show you where on the way out." Sabine had her assignment well laid out. She asked Victor how he and Rich would get aboard the yacht. The captain had it all figured out, "We will depart from across the inlet. A good friend of mine who lives here part-time lent me his ketch named Petit Canard (Little Duck.) He will have what we will need waiting for us on the boat." Victor lit up a Gitane, got in the front seat of the car, and pulled away slowly. Let's all go to your hotel and prepare the equipment. We have two hours to rest before the assault, which will take place around 2:30 a.m.

Rich did not mind having Victor in charge of the operation. The man was trained for the job, and most of all, he was familiar with the arbor.

CHAPTER 58

T HE PEUGEOT PULLED IN AND PARKED ABOUT A BLOCK from the hotel. While Sabine and Rich went over their guns and working clothes, Victor waited patiently, another Gitane hanging from his lips. To pass the time and keep everyone alert, Sabine prepared a pot of coffee and served sandwiches the couple had bought at the airport, just in case. The trio reviewed the final details of the upcoming storming of the Muhammad bin Salman in the Marseille harbor. Then Rich wiped down the handles and doorknobs, leaving no prints or personal items behind. Sabine and Victor returned to the vehicle while Rich walked around the block to ensure no one was roaming in the area. Victor did not pull away from the curb as expected. He addressed Sabine, "Make sure you do not kill the prince, if at all possible." At once, Rich and Sabine asked why. The explanation that Victor offered was coherent. "I have been thinking about what would happen if we killed the prince. You know the United States and the House of Saud are very close. One of your major oil companies is now in partnership with the Saudis on the stock market. "You remember 9-11, don't you? Almost all of the perpetrators were Saudis, and because of this special entente, exceptional understanding, and particular arrangement between the two countries, this crime was never explored. Killing the prince would create a grave situation for us, resulting in the US government chasing you and me to the end of the earth. Now all wound up, Victor deviated the conversation to air his thoughts regarding the CCC and the US government in general. "The CCC, you are fighting, they made billions from the Bush and Chenney alliance. The Vice President was running the country at the time. If you remember, France exposed the lies about the yellow cake and tried to stop the 2003 war in Iraq. The CCC came out a winner and is presently involved in feeding money to terrorists. In Europe, we have a good idea of what goes on in your congress, the CIA, etc."

He finally paused and said, "Let's drive to our launching spot." Victor threw in a few recommendations to Sabine, "Make sure you wipe all the prints off the bullets you put in your magazines and wipe your rifle off and throw it away in the deep water before leaving. It will take eight to ten minutes before any police show up at the Marseille-ile Ratonneau, the bridge across the inlet. Wipe your pistol and extra mags off and throw them in the bay along with your comms unit, which will have to be put inside a bag with a heavy rock. Oh, make sure you keep your gloves on to do all that." Sabine asked what else she had to do after receiving the order to return to the car. As decided earlier, she would have nothing else to do but go to the airport. "Find a bathroom so you can change, drop the car keys in the box at the car rental, and park the car. Take the 6:00 a.m. flight to Paris. As you know, you have a reservation— the thought of leaving her man behind worried her a little.

"Victor, I don't want Rich hurt, I count on you."

The agent shook his head and smiled, then said, "I am sure Vic has it all worked out, knowing him." To reassure her, Rich briefly went over the steps of the operation.

"We will drive to Le petit canard, the name of Vic's friend's ketch, and from there, swim to the yacht, eliminate a few vermins, and swim back. We will stay in touch until it is time for you to go." Vic added a few details to help put Sabine's mind at rest.

"We attack the ship around 3:00 a.m. We are aboard the yacht a maximum of ten, fifteen minutes. Swimming back to the boat will take close to forty minutes."

Rich had many questions of his own but knew it was best to say nothing in the company of Sabine. As Rich got up from his chair, he looked at Victor and said, "Isn't time to go?"

Few words exchanged as Victor drove back to the Vieux Port. But instead of going down the Q du Port this time, he made a left turn down the R Breteuil, then a quick right along the bay on the Quai de Rive Neuve.

A few minutes later, he pulled near the magnificent Jardin du Pharo, fifteen hundred acres of peaceful and natural garden where people love to stroll. To the right of it was an almost entirely closed bay. There seemed to be hundreds of small motorboats and yachts, and dozens and dozens of sailboats. Victor stopped,

"I am going to park here. Sabine, you leave your stuff in the trunk. Rich, you must bring all your gear with you."

As usual, Victor lit up one of his smelly Gitane cigarettes, and with the usual limp, he led them out along the array of crafts. It was not long before he stopped and pointed at a two-mast ketch—a wooden sailboat that was wider than the rest. Vick slowed down and pointed at the boat's name painted on one side of the watercraft, Petit Canard (little duck.)

Victor put out his cigarette and signaled for Sabine and Rich to follow him on board. Once inside the old but beautiful craft, Rich spotted two rebreathers and two wet suits."

"How did you get all this so fast?"

"I have friends in this area, one special one, the owner of this boat. We go back a long way. Remember, I was in the service here. I was young then."

"So we are going to swim from here to the yacht, do our things and swim back," Rich said.

"It is not that far." Victor looked at his watch and said, "Sabine, here is your comms unit, and Rich here is yours. Let's test them before she leaves." The three of them put their sets on; the gadgets worked fine." Then Victor said, "Sabine, I am sure you recognized the place at the end of the pier where you will be working from." She shook her head. Before Sabine departed, Rich hugged her for a long minute. Then Victor walked over, put his arms around her, and said, "We will be fine. I promise I will bring your man home to you. Won't be long before we see you in Paris in a day or two."

Several minutes later, Sabine contacted both Victor and Rich from her assigned location. The units worked perfectly. Rich still had a lot of recommendations to share with Sabine, "We will contact you before going aboard. Again, make sure the silencer screwed on tight. If your fire, fire twice, high in the chest. A small wave could cause the boat to list, or even the wind could cost you a headshot. Two 7.65 Nato rounds will leave a hole the size of a can of peas in the chest and probably pulverize the head. Remember, as soon as we tell you, head for the car and go directly to the airport. I will miss you."

CHAPTER 59

O N THE KETCH, RICH SAT DOWN AND PULLED ON HIS wet suit. Across from him, Victor was standing up, drawing on his hood. He pulled on his tight-fitting goggles, made sure they fitted properly, then lifted them so he could see clearly while speaking. "Rich, with your compass, go forward and take a reading of where the yacht is. When you come back, we will compare the numbers. Oh, and don't forget to figure our return reading."

While Rich was gone, Victor secured the weapons in two watertight bags. The second bag, a replacement, in case one got lost. Then he tied on a nylon rope to each bag, and last, he left one section of rope about twenty-five feet long lying on the floor. Just as Victor was securing his weights to his body, Rich walked back in.

"I came up with three-hundred and forty-two degrees going over. What did you get?"

"I had three-hundred and forty-nine. A distance so close makes no difference. There is a lot of metal around here to make the compass vary a little." After they compared their return headings, minus one-hundred and eighty degrees from their original direction, they went over the list of things they would do once onboard the yacht.

Rich secured his lead-weighted belt, and the two men strapped on knives to their calf, below the knee. Last, both of them stored watertight mini-mag flashlights inside a pocket on their vest. With their fins on, they walked backward onto the aft of the deck.

Rich reached over and picked up a rebreather and said, "Climb overboard, and I will hand it to you. That way, it will be less effort to put it on."

Vic looked at Rich with a frown on his face. "You young whippersnappers think I am too old. Well, old Victor is going to pull your ass to the yacht, you'll see." Victor picked up the rope that he had dropped on the floor earlier and tied it around his waist, then he said, "Now, you do the same thing with the other end of the rope, with it on, you won't get lost underwater." After laughing, Victor jumped into the bay. When his head came up, Rich handed him the rebreather.

With the rope around his waist, Rich jumped into the calm sea. After both men had their breathing devices in place and working, they gave each other the universal OK sign with their fingers.

CHAPTER 60

EVERY FIVE MINUTES, VIC WOULD CHECK HIS COMPASS'S glow, turn around and give Rich an OK sign. Once the water became just a bit more turbulent, he stopped and waited until Rich got closer. Vic signalled to go above water, and as the two men surfaced, Vic leaned over next to Rich's head and said, "I hear a boat coming. We need to recheck the compass heading; the result may have changed just a little. Rich spotted the boat coming from their right and going out to sea. Vic said, "It's now three hundred and forty-eight degrees. Go as deep as you can, so that fishing boat can maneuver above us."

Beneath the dark waters, it was eerie. The two men continued advancing for another half-hour. Then, almost like magic, they found themselves face to face with the hull of the yacht. Vic signalled Rich he was going to surface and wanted him to remain submerged. When he returned beneath the light waves, he pulled on the rope to have Rich follow him. Vic gave the one-finger pointed up to go to the surface. As their heads came out of the water, Victor pushed his goggles on his forehead, leaned over against Rich's ear, and said, "We are going to the right." Once the men were at the aft, they found a set of stairs and a rope hanging over the side of the craft, which Rich used to tie the waterproof bags containing the two sets of armory. The men took off their fins and placed them in one of the bags, along with their goggles and rebreathers. They snapped their lead belts to the stairs, just below the water surface.

The two partners hung their automatic rifles over their shoulders and placed their sidearms around their waist. Each one put extra mags and two packets of C4 with timers in his wet suit pocket. Victor handed Rich a comms unit, which they tested. Surprisingly a third voice, fresh, young, and feminine, came over the comms units saying, "In place, you are loud and clear, over."

Rich felt good knowing Sabine was keeping an eye on him and Victor. Feeling encouraged by the sound of his fiancee's voice, he said, "Going aboard in under five minutes. Sight-in your gun, out."

Then Rich was surprised when Vic took out a garrote made of a thin wire out of his pocket. The old man looked at Rich, then said, "It's light and doesn't take much room. Never leave home without it."

Rich climbed slowly up the vertical steel ladder hanging from the craft. As his head cleared the railing, he looked forward and on both sides. With his automatic rifle and silencer pointed forward, the gun looked like a small machine gun. Rich slid down behind an engine cover at the very rear of the ship.

Just as Victor's head appeared over the railing, a man fell forward in the semi-darkness of the doorway. Blood was pouring from two large wounds in his chest, and an automatic weapon laid at his side. Holding their breath, Victor and Rich realized that Sabine had spotted this individual with her night scope and had probably saved their lives. Sabine, the guardian angel, had been surveilling with extreme attention the two executioners' arrival onto the craft. Victor finished sliding over the railing as Rich spoke into his comms unit. "Thanks."

"Roger that."

The two men had decided to clear the yacht's starboard side, the side that Sabine could see. Rich worked his way forward first. About a minute later, he heard a scuffle. He stopped immediately, rotated to face the noise provenance, ready to fire his automatic weapon.

Nothing prepared Rich for the sudden presence of an individual kicking and now falling heavily to the floor. Blood was pouring out onto the deck as Victor's garrote had almost cut the guard's head off. Rich looked at the captain with a smile. Victor said, "I think they have a night watchman who monitors the activities on the decks. We must take him out now before we go farther." Then the older man reached inside his wet suit and pulled out a paper, a rough sketch of the craft. He studied it for a few seconds and said, "The guardhouse should be to the left just beside that bulkhead, right there, almost in front of us."

Rich spoke softly into his comms unit. "Going inside."

"Roger."

Rich dropped to his knees and, with his automatic rifle pointed forward, pulled the slightly open door. The office was empty. Rich walked inside the room as Victor stepped to the side. There was a door to the left, leading to another room with the light was on. Rich gingerly took a look inside through the door that had been left ajar. He saw a man with a headset sitting on a chair busy watching several monitors.

Victor moved back to speak into his comms unit, "Stay low, open door a little more, and I will put him to sleep."

When Rich pushed the door open, it gave off a slight rubbing noise. The guard immediately spun on his swivel chair. Victor instantly stepped into the room and fired. Even though he used a silencer, the pop sound was sharp and loud in the small watertight room, almost as loud as a 22 short firing. Blood and brain matter flew all over the monitors as the man fell to the floor.

Now inside the room, Rich and Victor looked at the monitors. Two armed men stood guard in the front of the yacht, one on each side. "We must exterminate them before we go below," Rich said.

"Let's look at the chart on the wall, and see where your two CCC friends are staying." Immediately, they spotted their names indicating their two rooms on deck two, just above where the galley was. Rich then said, "I would like to eliminate the head of security. Do you see his name, Dubois?" Victor studied the layout of the craft. "Ah, here it is. He stays one deck below here, and more guards have living quarters in three rooms down the passageway. Which ones do we eliminate first?"

Rich studied the guard rotation sheet posted next to the monitor. We better take out the guards working outside before we go after the essential targets who, I am sure, do not carry a firearm. The guards are all armed and could walk upon us at any time."

As the two men walked back outside, Rich spoke into his comms unit.

"Can you see any guards at the front of the ship?"

"Yes, on the starboard side. I have a clear shot."

"Stand down for now. We will go around the port side and try to take the other one out first."

"Roger that."

As the two men slowly moved in the dark along the deck, they kept their guns pointing forward. Suddenly, they saw a man sitting in a chair with his feet on the railing. Victor tapped Rich to get his attention. "No doubt, this man is a candidate for the garrote." Victor was about to sneak up behind the guard and use his favorite tool, the garrote, once again and leave a bloody mess on the deck. Quietly and vigilantly, they worked their way closer to the front. Then, out of the blue, without any warning, a guard jumped forward. As he pulled his gun up to fire, Rich shot him in the head. The man was dead before he hit the deck.

The guard on the starboard side had heard the silenced gunshot. He raised his automatic weapon and began to move toward the port side. Suddenly, he fell forward, and blood began to flow out from under his chest. "I had to take the shot," Sabine said over the comms unit.

"Roger that, and thanks," Rich said. "We are going inside. If not back outside in five minutes from now, you leave."

Victor and Rich worked their way down the passageway, then took the first set of steps up to the next deck. Rich opened a door and leaned over, with his gun pointed forward. Vic took a moment to look at the key numbers he had picked up in the guard room. Henri Dubois, the man in charge of security, was in suite 212, and Williams, in 213. Both partners hugged the bulkhead as they worked their way down the passageway. Vic stopped and pointed at the door marked 212. Just like two superbly trained SWAT members, they stood ready. Victor took out the first key and inserted it. The tumblers in the door turned with almost no sound. The door opened, Rich stepped inside, then Victor followed, closing the door behind himself. They moved like cats through the luxurious room. Henri Dubois was sleeping in the king-size bed, and against him was a lady whose arm rested across the gentleman's chest. The smell of alcohol was overwhelming.

Rich whispered into Victor's ear. "I will take a pillow and shoot him in the head. Be ready to put your hand over the woman's mouth, so we don't hear her screams. I don't want to shoot her."

Victor nodded and handed Rich a pillow. Rich placed the silencer deep into the large soft pillow and fired. The woman moved, and as she started to open her eyes, a rubber-gloved hand came down over her mouth. With little trouble, the two men tied her securely and placed a gag in her mouth. As they started to leave, Rich pointed to the white power spread out on the nightstand.

"Drunk and doped out of their head with coke," Victor said into his comms unit.

The two men closed the door behind them. Rich wondered if it would be as easy to kill Theodore Williams.

CHAPTER 61

THE TWO MEN LOOKED DOWN THE PASSAGEWAY BOTH ways. No one was aware of their presence on the yacht yet. Victor stuck his finger into his pocket and brought out the second key, checked the number on the door, and gave Rich an up and down movement with his head. Rich was closely watching Vic slide the key into the lock of room 213. Once again, they furtively moved into the room without a sound. They were somewhat amused when they came across one chubby naked woman with her right leg wrapped over Theodore's heavy thigh, and another female was sleeping against his back with her left arm resting on his fleshy upper arm. As they got closer, Victor, with a grimace on his face, pointed at the bare well-formed shiny butt. He looked at Rich and pretended to unzip his fly.

Back to business, Victor picked up a pillow from the floor and handed it to Rich. The situation was a little more complicated than usual; this time, the two partners had three individuals to bring under control without alarming others in the close vicinity.

Victor indicated with his gun that he would knock unconscious the ladies by hitting them on the head. The pillow came down on Williams's face, Rich fired. With tremendous speed, Victor's gun hammered the first lady, leaving no time for the second one to utter a word. The women would probably wake up with a severe headache, but they would be alive. Rich securely tied and gagged one of the ladies while Victor took his time immobilizing the other's flabby body. Now, with everyone was placid or dead, the partners took a few seconds to look around the room. Empty champagne bottles had rolled on the floor, and spilled cocaine was visible on both nightstands. The smell of alcohol, combined with the fragrance of heady perfume, filled the room's sultry air.

Mission having been accomplished in room 213, the two men left quietly. Rich stopped for a second; he wanted to kill the prince's head security guard. Victor touched Rich's arm, shook his head disapproving, then pointed the exit door to Rich. As he passed the guards' room where several of them were sleeping, Victor took out a small block of C4 and timer he sat at the bottom of the door.

Before leaving the inside passage, Vic stepped inside the security room that held all the computers, monitors, cameras, videos, and one dead guard, their first victim, who was still on the floor. Vic took out the second block of C4, set another timer in the room. Without incident, they were soon back on the main deck. Rich spoke to Sabine into his comms unit, "We are back on the main deck. Give us cover until we go overboard, then get the hell out of here. Love you."

"Roger that."

As Victor was climbing down the stairs into the water, his partner stood guard. Rich had just put his foot on the ladder when, out of nowhere, a man came into view. While the agent brought up his weapon, the guard fired, and the bullet burned across Rich's left shoulder. The man was not so lucky. He stumbled forward with blood pouring from his chest. Without warning, another man, and a second one, appeared. Rich fired, and each guard received two bullets each in the torso. Blood was flowing everywhere. In the meantime, Victor was preparing the gear left behind before the attack back in the water. Rich ordered Vic to go as he was dropping into the water, "Leave now, go, go, go."

Now underwater, Rich held his breath as he snapped on his weight belt and slid his mouth over the mouthpiece. Following Vic closely, he tied on the rope to his belt. The partners had another challenging forty-five-minute swim ahead of them.

As they swam along, a loud and blunt noise was heard beneath the water, immediately followed by water turbulence that tossed the two men around. Rich wondered what was going on. Victor never panicked; he knew this commotion was caused by the explosion of one of the two blocks C4 he had strategically placed on the yacht. With the second explosion, they were hit with another powerful wave. The vessel was now illuminated, and guards were running and shouting.

On land, Sabine had discarded the gun and mags in the sea. She had returned to the car and was on her way to the airport. Sirens could be heard in the distance.

Rich could not see Victor up ahead of him, but the rope stayed taut.

The visibility was low; there was no time or distance. The men depended on the compass heading in those dark waters. Soon, with their heads raised just above the surface, they discovered they were now inside the protected bay. Vic took a reading on the ketch and sank beneath the water once again to reemerge right away.

Rich said, "What the hell happened back there? That was quite a wham." The agent had not seen his partner dropping blocks of C4 in two locations. "I left the guards a going-away present, two blocks of C4. We are going to drop our guns here. Take off your suit and tie your weighted belt around it and let it sink. We will swim back to the Little Duck, the ketch, in our shorts." Now back on the boat, the two men were shivering. After drying off, they put their street clothes back on.

Monaco is a sovereign country, the second smallest globally, but it has some five hundred police officers and even an army of 82. One could hear the musical sound of sirens and see the flashing lights of the police cars rushing to the dock closest to the prince's yacht. Ambulances followed, causing a deafening cacophony at dawn.

Due to the prince's diplomatic immunity, the local Monegasque police would treat the situation with kid gloves. Still, due to the several murders aboard, they would investigate without upsetting the wealthy prince. His visits to Monaco were too profitable to the small country.

"I wonder if Sabine got away OK," Rich said.

"She is one hell of a sniper, and I am glad she is on our team. She had plenty of time to get to the airport. All she had to do was drop the car keys and leave the car. She will be fine."

When finally dressed, the men wiped the deck and inside the boat. They rang out their shorts and took them along to be discarded elsewhere. Victor lit a Gitane, took a few puffs, and watched the light show across the small bay. "We need to go soon as the police will be closing off the streets. About one and a half kilometers from here, near the Abbaye St-Victor, we will catch a city bus. I recommend we avoid leaving the city by plane or on the train. The police will be on alert."

"I better break my phone apart and start throwing pieces away."

"You can throw some in the bay here. As we go along, we'll get rid of the rest. Let's hurry, but let's not look suspicious."

CHAPTER 62

S ABINE SPENT CONSIDERABLE TIME WIPING DOWN THE Peugeot as she did not want anyone's print left inside or outside the vehicle. She wiped off the keys, dropped them in the night return box, and headed for the Marseille Provence Airport entrance. Once inside the building, Sabine spent some time in the first ladies' restroom available. Sabine applied cold water to her face and hands and put on a clean blouse and skirt. After combing her hair, she put on some makeup to hide the dark rings under her eyes. After all, Sabine had not slept in over twenty hours. At the Air France ticket counter, she was all smiles and bubbly when the agent handed her one-way ticket to Charles de Gaulle airport in Paris. Waiting patiently for the embarkation time, Sabine started to worry about her man, wondering if he was hurt or worse. There was no way to contact him. Once in her first-class seat on the plane, she began to relax.

In Marseille, two men stepped onto their second bus ride of the morning, traveling into the city's outskirts. Victor had plans. As the bus moved toward its next stop, the old captain said, "There is a used car lot not too far from here. With enough cash, we could buy silence and a vehicle to get us to Toulon."

"What is there in Toulon that will help us?" Rich replied with edginess.

"If you like history, there is a lot to see and do in Toulon; unfortunately, we are on the run. Just one interesting point, Toulon has been a military harbor since the 1400s, the French navy has been based at Toulon for more than 500 years. Once there, we will buy a small suitcase, act like tourists, and catch a bus ride to Ales, and from Ales, one last bus transfer to Paris."

Once the bus pulled in Toulon, Rich purchased a burner phone to call Sabine from Ales.

CHAPTER 63

J UST BEFORE THE BUS PULLED OUT OF ALES, RICH CALLED Sabine. After the fifth ring, he heard her soft sensual voice greeting him, "Bonjour. I am so glad to hear your voice. Where are you?"

Rich did not wish to go over any detail concerning the journey, "We are on our way home and should be there late tonight. Everything is fine. We enjoyed our trip on the water, and we came across quite a few travelers." After several more carefully chosen words, Rich terminated the call. The partners did not feel free or safe to add more, but hearing each other's voice reassured them.

Hours later, before the bus pulled into Paris, Rich called her with the approximative arrival time. Since Victor and Rich would be catching a cab, no meeting place needed to be given over the phone.

When Victor and Rich arrived at Marguerite's apartment where Sabine was staying, hugs and kisses were exchanged. Now free to say anything, the trio joyfully shared what happened the night before and throughout the day. At last, Sabine could enjoy talking to her man. She noticed Rich repeatedly nursing his left shoulder with his right hand, the site of a minor injury sustained while leaving the yacht. He explained the graze was insignificant and required no treatment, but she insisted on seeing the scrape.

The trio enjoyed a glass of chilled rose that the hostess served with mixed nuts. It was getting late when Sabine said, "I think we should go and have dinner. I slept part of the day, I was too tired to prepare anything for dinner, and I had no idea when you would arrive. I know just the place where we should celebrate the successful operation. We will have dinner on the river Seine where I had my first dinner date with Rich."

The two men who had spent the entire day traveling on buses took a quick shower, and once ready, jumped in Sabine's little car.

After the bottle of champagne was uncorked, and the glasses filled, Rich said, "I would like to make a toast to the woman I love, and to a man I did not know a week ago. A man I would go to hell and back with." After the glasses clicked, and the palates soaked with the bubbly, Rich continued. "Victor, when Sabine and I get married, would you be my best man?"

The captain got up, saluted, then hugged Rich. "Old Victor was honored to work with you. Count on me, I will be there for the wedding, and I will be happy to reconnect with my friend Andy. Should you come across another assignment, you will make old Vic happy if you chose him to assist you."

At the restaurant, the trio laughed and talked until the waiter brought their dinner. To celebrate the mission's end, they ordered three identical meals consisting of duck liver pâté, warm goat cheese on a mixed green salad, and for entree, scallops cooked in garlic and tomato bits served with risotto. They all chose a simple crème brûlée for dessert and a cup of coffee to complete this feast.

After the champagne, the server suggested the guests drink a Sancerre, a white wine from the Loire Valley, "a food-friendly" wine, according to the waiter.

Back in the car, they buckled up. Sabine reached under her seat and brought out Le Figaro's copy, the French newspaper's afternoon edition. "I need to read you something before we head home." The two men became quiet and listened with attention, wondering if the article in the paper she was about to share with them was linked to the assault on the yacht anchored in Marseille. "The Rothchild family will be sending Andrew Rothchild the fifth on business to the United States in September. His appointment will involve the installation of a natural gas pipeline in Saudi Arabia. The project will include Chevron's participation, the American multinational energy corporation, and another unnamed Texas oil company. Following a recent incident in Marseille, the Rothchild envoy will be provided heavy security. Victor and Rich stared at each other. Both had a silly grin on their face.

Victor responded, «Je voulais toujours voir les États-Unis. (I always wanted to visit the United States.) Here is my chance." Rich did not respond because, at this precise moment, he wanted to stay away from dangerous situations and enjoy a peaceful existence with Sabine. A bluish cloud of cigarette smoke started drifting all over the car.